CANDLELIGHT ROMANCES™

Return To Love

Beverly Sommers

A CANDLELIGHT ROMANCE™

Published by
Dell Publishing Co., Inc.
1 Dag Hammarskjold Plaza
New York, New York 10017

Dell ® TM 681510, Dell Publishing Co., Inc.

Candlelight Romance™ is the trademark of
Dell Publishing Co., Inc., New York, New York

ISBN: 0-440-17543-7

Printed in the United States of America
First printing—January 1982

Chapter One

I still have occasional nightmares and wake up to the sound of the ocean. It's a different ocean though, and a different sound. Instead of crashing waves against the rocky coast of Massachusetts, I now hear gentle waves breaking along the beach, and they usually lull me back to sleep. The nightmares are of that other coast three thousand miles away, and while they never change, in time they have grown less frequent, and my husband tells me that someday they will be completely forgotten. But I don't think such events are ever forgotten, not when they involve fear and horror and even death.

It began just about a year ago on an otherwise very ordinary day. It was the beginning of July, and in Southern California one summer day is very much like the next. We don't get thunderstorms or sudden spells of either cold or hot weather. At the beach it's either overcast in the morning or not; the afternoons are always sunny, the evenings cool. Unlike other parts of the country, the weather is monotonous, but monotonously nice. I was a schoolteacher—high school English—and so was off for the summer. Except for a couple of graduate courses I was taking toward my master's degree at the state college, I spent most of my time at the beach. I read there and wrote poetry, studied for my classes, met friends for picnic lunches, joined in occasional games of volleyball, and, of course, swam a lot. In short, most of my summer social life revolved around the beach.

Apartments in Seal Beach being expensive, I had a roommate, Cindy Bolen, whom I had gone to college with and who was then a counselor at Juvenile Hall.

Every morning, understandably enough, she begrudged the fact that I could stay in bed while she had to go to work, and that morning was no exception. She made so much noise banging cupboards in the kitchen, that I finally gave up trying to go back to sleep and got out of bed.

It was overcast and cool, but I bundled up in my chenille robe and carried a cup of coffee and the *Los Angeles Times* out onto the sun deck and tried to catch a glimpse of the ocean through the fog.

"You got some mail, Katie," Cindy called out to me before she left, but I was busy perusing the movie section of the paper, feeling in the mood to see a foreign film that night, and didn't immediately go inside to get it.

When my robe began to get damp from the fog, I went back inside for a second cup of coffee. The letter was on the kitchen table, looking innocuous enough, until I picked it up and recognized the writing as Susan's—my sister. My twin sister, actually, and identical at that. I felt a twinge of guilt with the realization that for long periods of time I actually forgot I had a sister. And that was quite a feat, considering that for the better part of my life I was not allowed to forget it for a moment.

I also felt surprise as I ripped open the envelope. For five years, ever since Susan's precipitous trip back East and her subsequent marriage, all I had received from her were Christmas cards. After my first few attempts at correspondence with her had been rebuffed, I too had slid into the habit of merely exchanging Christmas cards with a brief note added.

The letter was short and would have been alarming from anyone but my sister. But knowing her proclivity for the dramatic, I merely raised an eyebrow before putting the kettle on to boil. When I had settled down at the table with my coffee, I read it again.

"Dear Kathryn," it began. My friends all called me Katie, but never my sister. "I tried to call you, but the operator wouldn't give me your number. You've got to help me, Kathryn. Please come here—right away. Rick hates me! I'm afraid!! I'm so afraid!!!!" And then her sprawling signature. The quotation marks were pure Susan, as was the brevity.

I hadn't thought that she might want to reach me when Cindy and I had requested an unlisted telephone number. Both of us had constantly been besieged by unwanted phone calls, and we had finally, in desperation, changed the number and had it unlisted, giving it out only to friends and, in Cindy's case, to her family.

And so, when the phone rang a few minutes later and a voice I had clearly not forgotten said, "This is Rick Allison," the first thing I said was, "How did you get my number?"

There was a pause. "From the college. The registrar's office had it—said you were taking classes this summer. Listen, Kathryn—"

"It's funny your calling," I interrupted him. "I just got a letter from Susan, saying she tried to call me."

"Listen to me, Kathryn," he said, his voice harsh and impatient. "I don't quite know how to tell you this, but there isn't really an easy way. Your sister is dead."

It didn't penetrate at first. I was half listening and half wiping up the coffee I had spilled while answering the phone, and thinking how I'd know his voice anywhere, even after five years.

"Did you hear me, Kathryn? Susan's dead."

When the news did penetrate, it didn't seem real. It was as if I were watching television and it was happening to someone on a show. Then I remembered when Susan and I had been told of our parents' death in a plane crash. We had been twelve at the time, old enough to understand, but we had gone right on playing, confident our mother would be home soon to fix dinner. It wasn't until a neighbor took us over to her house to eat that night that it began to seem real for us, and we finally broke down and cried.

Now I was the last one left of the whole family, and I didn't want to be that alone.

"It's not possible," I protested weakly. "She's not old enough to die."

"Kathryn." His voice was gentle now. "Do you have someone there who can be with you?"

"How did she die? Tell me how she died."

"I'd rather not—"

"Tell me how she died," I demanded, wanting to know it all so that I could make some sense of it.

"It appears she killed herself, Kathryn."

I was crying now and shivering all over, despite the fact that the sun had dissipated the fog and was now flooding the kitchen with warm sunlight.

"What do you mean, it appears?" I said, choking over the words. "How did she die?"

He hesitated a moment while I clasped my robe more tightly around me. "She went over the cliff. Her body was found this morning on the beach." And then, as though reading my thoughts, he added, "But it couldn't have been an accident. There's a guardrail at the point at which she went off."

I was taking deep breaths in an effort to calm myself. "She wouldn't have killed herself, not ever. I know that as surely as I know I'm standing here." And I did know it. Susan was capable of destroying lives around her, but not her own. Selfish people don't kill themselves.

"Kathryn, perhaps I should call you back later."

"I'm flying out there. Today."

"That's not necessary, Kathryn." He sounded surprised. Perhaps he thought the lack of communication between Susan and me had been my doing.

"It's necessary to me," I told him.

He was silent for a moment. "I'll meet you at the airport in Boston. Call me back and let me know your arrival time."

"Don't bother. I'll rent a car," I said. I hung up then, not even saying good-bye. I had talked as long as I could; I needed time to think.

Then I saw her letter on the table, completely forgotten when Rick had broken the news to me. My mind wasn't yet ready to relate her letter to her death, but I folded it up and put it in my purse which was hanging over one of the kitchen chairs.

I called the airport and reserved a flight to New York. I would have an hour's layover there before getting a connecting flight to Boston. I then called Sandra, one of my friends who taught with me at Marina High School, and she agreed to drive me to the airport.

I had only an hour to get ready before she was to pick me up, but I had choosen that flight so I wouldn't have time to sit around and think.

I called Cindy at work and told her what had happened. She burst into tears, but they were for me, I knew, and not Susan, whom she had never liked.

"I'll come right home, hon. You shouldn't be alone."

"No, Cindy, I'm flying there in a couple of hours. I should be back in a day or two. If I let you know when, would you pick me up?"

"Of course I'll pick you up. Do you need any money?"

I didn't have much, but I had credit cards. "No, I'm okay."

"Well, if you want to take any of my clothes, help yourself."

I made the call short, knowing personal calls at work could get Cindy in trouble. And I didn't feel like talking.

I didn't pack much, not planning on staying long: a pair of cotton pajamas and my robe, some underwear, and my one dark cotton dress that I sometimes wore to school functions and that would be suitable, I thought, for a funeral. I was planning on wearing jeans and a T-shirt and my running shoes to fly in. Not the most sophisticated gear for flying, but the most comfortable for the drive after I reached Boston. Anyway, there was no one I was trying to impress. Certainly not Rick Allison.

I went into the bathroom and took a shower and washed my hair. As I stood in front of the mirror, blowing my hair dry, I took a good look at myself. I didn't look grief-stricken, only tired. My eyes were a little bloodshot, which often happened when the smog came this far south. Other than that, I looked pretty good. I always do in the summer.

I have the kind of hair that's called dishwater-blond, although Susan always insisted on calling it ash-blond. In the winter, with my hazel eyes and pale skin, I always

10

think I look colorless—or all of a color. And so I wear blush and some eyeshadow and stay away from clothes in vivid colors. But in the summer my hair gets sun-streaked, and my skin turns a golden brown, making my eyes more green than hazel, and I know I look my best then.

I don't wear any makeup in the summer, just a little lip gloss to keep my lips from drying out, so it didn't take me long to get ready. In the time remaining before Sandra arrived, I called the college and spoke to the dean, explaining that I'd be missing a couple of classes. Then I watered my plants. Cindy would have done it, I was sure, but I wanted to talk to them and tell them to keep up the good work until I returned. I don't know if it helps or not, talking to plants, but I figured it couldn't hurt. And my plants all thrived, even the African Violets, and everyone else I knew had trouble with them.

When Sandra arrived, she put on her "mother" act, making me check to see if I had everything I needed, fussing around the apartment, locking doors and windows —something Cindy and I never bothered with—until I reminded her I only had forty minutes to catch my plane.

Since it was the middle of the day, the San Diego Freeway wasn't crowded, and we made good time despite Sandra's mode of driving, which was to get in the right lane and never move out of it. Normally this alone would have annoyed me, but at the same time she kept reminiscing about Susan in such a way that in retrospect my sister sounded like a saint, and this also bothered me. I knew that Sandra meant well, but I also knew that she had detested my sister.

When we got to the airport, I told Sandra not to bother parking, that there was no need for her to see me off, so she just pulled up in front of the airline terminal and put the car in neutral before turning to me.

She reached out and gave me a hug, her eyes brimming with tears, as were mine. "Listen, Katie, is there anything you need? Anything I can do for you?"

I shook my head. "You already have, Sandra. I really appreciate your bringing me here. I should be back in a couple of days."

The last thing she said to me was, "Be careful, huh?" as I got out of the car. And I wished then that I had been able to say the same to my sister. If I had, perhaps she would still have been alive.

Chapter Two

Los Angeles International wasn't as hectic as usual, despite all the tourists, and I picked up my ticket and boarded my flight quickly. Lunch was served as soon as we were airborne, and afterward a movie was shown. It wasn't one I would normally have chosen to see, but it distracted me, which was what I wanted at the moment.

The stopover in New York was a bore, and the flight to Boston short and uneventful. At the airport I rented a Monza, good on gas but without the power I liked.

Walking out of the air terminal into the parking lot, I received my first shock. Humidity was something we seldom experienced in California, and never like that of Boston. I felt as though I had walked into a steam bath. But my car was blessedly air-conditioned, and by the time I had sat in it and figured out my route on the road map I had been provided with, the interior of the car was cool and I was ready to set off.

Rick Allison lived in Cauley, a bare pinpoint on the map. It appeared to be part of the section called Cape Ann. The drive was longer than I had anticipated, but I love to drive and didn't mind. I needed time to think and I was in no hurry to see Rick again.

The scenery was lovely, what I noticed of it; I kept my

eyes on the road most of the time. There was lots of greenery—something I wasn't used to—and the bridges I frequently crossed actually had water under them, unlike the dry riverbeds of California. But my mind wasn't on the countryside. I had put off thinking about my sister's death and Rick Allison, but I felt I had to clear my head before I reached his house.

Since my sister's letter had preceded her death so closely, I was not able to attribute its hysterical tone simply to her overly dramatic nature. She had said she was afraid; that Rick hated her. But she had died, and Rick had said it was suicide. The letter didn't sound suicidal, just desperate, and I would never have believed Susan capable of suicide anyway. But then I wouldn't have believed Rick capable of killing her, either, a suspicion I was forced to consider, as I really didn't know much about him.

I had met Rick Allison before Susan had met him. We were nineteen then, Susan and I, and sophomores at college. With the trust that had been set up for us after our parents' deaths, we were able to move out on our own after high school, and we shared a small one-bedroom apartment near Long Beach City College, where I was majoring in English and planning on getting a secondary school credential in order to teach. Susan was majoring in drama, but I never knew why. She didn't like to study, but I supposed she thought it would be an easy major.

I met Rick between Christmas and New Year's at a party that was given by the head of the English department. Rick was on campus that semester as a visiting author, giving a graduate seminar in creative writing. I had read both his books, the first a war story set in Vietnam, and the second a novel with an academic back-

14

ground, reputedly Harvard. The party was in his honor which was the only reason I had gone. I knew he was teaching at Long Beach City College, but I had never seen him on campus, and being a great admirer of his novels, I longed to at least get a look at him.

But I was out of my element at the party. I was the only one there who wasn't either a faculty member or a graduate student. I didn't know anyone well enough to talk to, and I was much too shy to start a conversation with someone I didn't know. After awhile, feeling very out of place and having given up on the author's ever arriving, I wandered away from the living room and went down the hall until I came to a small book-filled study where I stepped inside to get a closer look. He was seated in a deep leather chair, and I recognized him at once from his picture on book jackets. I quickly turned to go, hoping to escape his notice. I had wanted to get a look at him, perhaps hear him speak, but I didn't want to disturb him, since he had obviously gone there to be alone.

"Don't run away. You're like a breath of spring on this otherwise dismal winter day." His voice was low and resonant with just enough of a New England accent to make it distinctive.

I stopped and laughed at that. "A dismal winter day? I thought you were from the East." The sun was out, and it was in the seventies; we were having a very warm winter that year. My dress was rather summery, but I couldn't bear to dress in winter wools when it was so warm out, and I suppose that is what he meant by a breath of spring.

He got up slowly from his chair, and I saw that he was several inches taller than me, although I'm not short. "You're right, it's not a dismal day at all," he said, smiling down at me. "And much too nice to waste on a boring

15

cocktail party. What would you say to playing hooky with me? Would you like to take a drive down the coast?"

It was like something out of a book, not at all the kind of ordinary thing that usually happened to me. I considered his offer briefly, then nodded my head yes.

He took my hand and led me out sliding glass doors and onto a patio that went around the house, ending in the circular driveway, where his car was parked. It was a bright-yellow Porsche, the top of which was down. He opened the door for me, and I slid into the passenger seat, thinking that the car didn't quite suit him. We had played a game at school, one popular in California, where everyone drives a car, of guessing from people's appearances what kind of car they own. The Porsche was nice, but I thought a Ferrari would have suited him better—something long and sleek, more like a racing car.

The rest of the day was like a dream, so totally perfect that sometimes I think I must have imagined it. He took the Pacific Coast Highway south, driving skillfully and with as much speed as possible, considering the amount of Sunday drivers.

We stopped at the Hungry Pelican in Newport Beach and had beers and roast beef sandwiches made on thick French bread, and talked of books and writing and colleges. At first he did most of the talking, but he soon drew me out, and I was talking as freely as I would to a close friend. I even admitted to him that I wrote poetry, and he told me he had started out writing poetry, too. We talked about our favorite poets, and he quoted some poetry to me, his voice sending shivers down my spine.

When we left the restaurant, I was afraid he'd head back to Long Beach, but he turned south again, and I breathed a sigh of relief. I never wanted the day to end. Farther south he drove over the bridge to Balboa Island, telling me it was one of his favorite spots, and we spent an hour walking around the shops.

In the bookstore he bought me a journal with a leather cover. "Poets should also keep journals," he said when he presented it to me, and I felt honored that he took my writing seriously.

We went as far as Laguna Beach that day. He parked the car, and we went down steep steps to the beach, where we took off our shoes and walked along the shore. He told me it was the only beach in Southern California that reminded him of home because of the rugged rock formations and the cliffs along which houses were built. The rest of Southern California's coastline is flat, with nothing of the wildness about it that Laguna's has.

When it started to get dark, he took me to Victor Hugo's for dinner. Of course I fell in love. It seemed natural at the time, and I suppose, given the romantic circumstances and my awe of him, inevitable. I had dated, of course, but usually young men my age. Rick's sophistication and soaring mind were new territory for me, territory I found myself wanting to explore. I liked his looks, too, which seemed to me rather "eastern" as opposed to the sunny blonds I was used to. His dark hair was worn rather shorter than was the style in California then, and the horn-rimmed glasses he used for driving shadowed his eyes that were like the gray of the ocean on a stormy day. But I think the most striking quality about him was his seemingly total ease with himself and his surroundings. He had a self-confidence that I lacked, and I envied him.

I wasn't experienced enough to act cool about what I was feeling, and I'm sure my adoration was plain to see in my eyes. My gaze rarely left his face.

He held my hand on the long ride home, and even though the night was cool and the top was down, I felt enveloped in warmth.

When he stopped in front of my apartment building, I remained seated in the car, my eyes on him, willing him to take me in his arms and kiss me. But he didn't. He reached out a hand and pushed my wind-tangled hair back from my face.

"Thank you for the day, sunshine," he said to me, and I reluctantly got out of the car and went up the stairs to the apartment. He had called me sunshine all day; he hadn't even asked me my name. But then I doubted I'd ever see him again, except perhaps in passing on the campus. He was older than me; he probably hadn't found me interesting at all, and anyway, the college frowned on teachers going out with students. He didn't seem rebellious enough to me to go against such strictures, although I wouldn't have thought I was, either. But I would have risked expulsion to see him again.

Susan must have noticed my euphoric state when I got in that night, because she turned off the TV and gave me her undivided attention. This was unusual for her; generally she found anything I did of no consequence at all. And because I was bursting to tell someone about Rick, and Susan was flattering me with her attention, I told her all about my newfound love.

She looked a bit skeptical when I had finished. "He's really that great, huh?"

"Oh, yes," I breathed. "He's perfect—at least for me."

"Well, you've never been hard to please," she said to me, turning the television back on and appearing to be engrossed in it. But from time to time that evening I felt her eyes on me as I sat studying at the desk.

18

My state of euphoria lasted a scant week. The following Saturday night Susan was mysterious about where she was going, and when I woke up Sunday to find that her bed had not been slept in, I was rather worried. Not that it hadn't happened before. On occasion when I would ask her where she was going or what time she would be back, she would tell me it was none of my business and to stop acting like a mother. I couldn't help it, though; there was a reckless side to Susan that was foreign to me, and I did worry about her.

She breezed in about four that afternoon. When I heard her on the stairs, I grabbed a book and pretended an unconcern I didn't feel.

She appraised me with a knowing look. "You were right; he *is* marvelous," she said to me in triumphant tones. I must have turned pale, because she gave a malicious laugh. "Oh, Kathryn, you didn't think you'd get him for yourself, did you? He's too much man for you, take my word for it. He thought you were silly and naive, but he thinks I'm a real woman."

I was confused, ashamed, and jealous. I shouldn't have been surprised. Susan had always gone after what I wanted, and her rate of success was high. What hurt the most was that he had discussed me with her, had told her that he found me silly.

First love does not die easily. The end of the semester was approaching, and I should have been studying hard for my exams, but my heart was broken and I couldn't seem to concentrate. I didn't even notice what Susan was doing during that time. I withdrew into myself, nursing my hurt. The only visible outcome of this was my poor showing when grades came out.

Rick was due to leave at the end of the semester, and

I had no reason to believe he would stay. If Susan was suddenly home more often and acting different, I didn't notice. I found myself avoiding her. I began doing most of my studying at the library, staying out late every night so that she would be asleep by the time I got home, and leaving the apartment in the morning before she got up. We had never spent much time together anyway, so I'm not sure she was even aware of what I was doing.

A few weeks later, when I came home one day to find that Susan had packed her clothes and moved out, I felt a sense of relief. After not hearing from her for several weeks, I found another student to share the expenses of the apartment with me and began to direct all my energies to my school work. The announcement that arrived in the mail, telling me of her marriage to Rick, didn't even upset me, at least not visibly. I sent a letter to her, which she never answered.

From a very early age Susan had resented being a twin. She had longed to be unique, one of a kind, but I was always around to remind her that she wasn't. It never bothered me as much, but then she always had the stronger personality. She was the outgoing one, bolder than I was with people, always wanting everything for herself and not liking to share. Visually, however, we were identical, and try as she would to look different, people always mistook us for one another.

Strangely enough, after she was gone, I found that I liked being the only one around, and I began to understand her attitude a little better. But I still felt a certain closeness to her, and it was somehow reassuring to know that I had a sister, even though she was three thousand miles away. Despite everything, she was my only living relative, and I would have hated to completely lose touch with her.

The thought of losing touch with her had brought me quickly out of my reverie, because after her death, of course, we would be forever out of touch. For the first time I really felt her death. And mourned her. I hoped that what I had once felt for Rick would not be revived when I saw him again. I was suspicious of him, deeply suspicious of the facts surrounding my sister's death, and I wanted to be able to view him objectively, feeling no more or less toward him than I would a stranger.

I made only two stops along the way, one at a hamburger stand for a drink, and later, when I got to Cauley, I stopped at a gas station to fill up and ask directions to Rick's house. Since he was a well-known writer, I assumed he would be something of a local celebrity. I was right. The boy at the gas station knew where his house was and gave me detailed directions on how to get there.

Cauley's main street was lined with quaint little shops, a couple of lovely old churches, and an inn that looked as though it had been built in Revolutionary times.

I switched off the air conditioner and rolled down my window as I turned off the main road and drew closer to the ocean. The air was cooler and less humid. There were large old houses set far apart and mailboxes strung along the road. I watched for one saying "Allison," and when I saw it, I pulled into the long unpaved driveway that led up to the house.

I parked in front, noting three other cars there, and turned off the ignition. I had always wondered what Rick's house would look like, but somehow I had pictured something more modern, all glass, wood, and sleek, low lines. This was a large rambling house of white clapboard with shutters painted dark green, and I looked it over with pleasure. I could see white ruffled curtains at the windows and a long screened-in porch along the whole front of the house.

I began to lose my courage then and almost turned the car around in an attempt to escape having to see Rick again. It wouldn't be a romantic meeting, not under the circumstances, and I was suddenly afraid of what I might find out. I told myself not to be such a coward; that I had come three thousand miles because my sister had died under mysterious circumstances, and if I left then I would never know what had really happened to her.

Taking my overnight bag with me, I got out of the car and approached the house. The screen door was open, and I went inside the porch and rang the doorbell. I could hear it chime inside and looked around the porch while I waited for someone to answer it. There was a glider and a lot of wicker furniture painted white, and I found it charming. I could hear voices, but no one came to the door, so I decided to walk around to the back to see if they were there.

The property was full of trees, bushes, and flower beds, and when I rounded the house, I just had time before I was noticed to note that there were several people sitting around a brick terrace. And then a shrill voice screamed, "Mommy!" and a small child with a head of dark curls came hurtling toward me and grabbed me by the legs.

Chapter Three

When I looked up from the child, the people were all on their feet, staring at me in different states of shock. A young woman about my age who looked rather like Rick walked over to me.

"Susan?" she asked me in a tentative voice, and I started thinking that perhaps a mistake had been made, that Susan wasn't dead after all.

I shook my head. "No, I'm her sister. Weren't you expecting me?"

The child, a girl, was still by my side, so I lifted her up and carried her over to where Rick was still standing, almost frozen, a look of incomprehension on his face. Then it dawned on me belatedly that the child had called me Mommy. "Am I an aunt?" I asked him. "I hadn't known that."

Rick looked as though he had received too many shocks that day. Or else he had aged more since his marriage than I would have thought possible. He looked thinner, his cheekbones were hollow, and there were dark circles under his eyes. He reached out to take the child, but she clung to me tightly, and his arms fell to his sides. "That's your aunt Kathryn, Sara, not your mother."

The child leaned back in my arms and studied my face.

She had her mother's big eyes and small nose, but her coloring was her father's. She was an adorable child, and I smiled down at her with pleasure. And then, strangely enough, I saw a hesitant look appear in her eyes at the sight of my smile. It was as if, my appearance to the contrary, she knew her mother wouldn't smile at her in such a way, and I wondered what damage Susan had inflicted upon her child in so short a time. Sara wiggled in my arms, and I set her down and watched as she moved to her father's side.

Rick seemed to remember the proprieties then and introduced me to the others. The young woman was his sister, Carol, the older couple his parents, and the good-looking blond man with the deep tan, looking more like a Californian than an easterner, was Dr. Paul Sanders, presumably the family doctor.

Carol drew me over to a chair next to hers and voiced what the others were surely thinking. "I'm sorry, Kathryn, it was just such a shock to us. We knew Susan had a sister, but she seldom mentioned you, and never that you were twins. It was like a ghost suddenly appearing."

I gave her a rueful look. "I'm not surprised. Susan never liked being a twin. And she never told me about Sara. But Rick had met me in California; he must have known we were twins." I looked over at Rick and saw that my words had only confused him further.

"I'm sorry, Kathryn," he said in a level tone. "I don't recall meeting you."

I'm sure I flushed at his remark, because he looked away from me, and I hope no one saw how distressed I was at his words. He had completely forgotten what for me had been the most memorable day of my life, and it was all I could do not to dissolve into tears at the realization.

The doctor offered me a vodka collins, which I accepted gratefully, and Rick's parents made polite conversation with me about my trip and where I lived in California. It seemed that Mrs. Allison's brother had retired to Palm Springs, where they frequently visited him, and, being avid golfers, they loved the area.

"Do you play golf, Kathryn?" Mr. Allison asked me.

"No, I'm afraid not. Just tennis. And call me Katie, please, everyone does."

"Oh, good, I need a tennis partner," said Carol, and, while we talked of tennis, I momentarily forgot that I was not there for a vacation and that there were more serious matters to discuss. But I sensed that they were keeping the conversation away from my sister's death for Sara's sake, and I agreed with that.

I felt Rick's eyes on me from time to time, and it made me nervous. When Carol suggested I might like to see my room and freshen up a bit before dinner, I quickly concurred, wanting a few moments alone to think about all that had happened. I also realized that the others were rather formally dressed and that my jeans and T-shirt weren't appropriate for the occasion.

Carol led me upstairs to a charming back bedroom that I loved at first sight. It had maple furniture, a bed with a yellow ruffled canopy and spread, and its own small adjoining bathroom. I expressed my delight, and Carol smiled, saying, "It was mine when I was young; Rick and I grew up in this house. My parents wanted something smaller and easier to take care of, so Rick bought it from them when he sold his first book. They have a condominium in town now."

I asked where she lived, and she told me in Boston,

where, like me, she was a teacher, only she taught deaf children in a special school there.

She was a nice girl, friendly and sweet, and I wondered if she and Susan had been friends. But Susan had never had girl friends, having always seen other girls as competition, so I didn't ask Carol for fear of embarrassing her.

I was sweaty and dusty from the long ride and took a shower before dressing in the navy cotton dress I had brought along for the funeral. I had told Carol that I had packed quickly and hadn't brought many clothes, and she suggested I help myself to Susan's. I decided the shock of my appearance was enough without adding to it by wearing Susan's clothes.

The room had a chaise longue, covered in flowered chintz, and I rested on it for a while before going downstairs to join the others. I was realizing already that I had probably made a mistake in coming East. The years had not lessened Rick's ability to affect me. His gaze alone was enough to shatter my composure. Added to that was the nagging thought that he had been a little too eager for me to believe my sister had committed suicide. Surely he had known Susan as well as I had; known that she was incapable of suicide. And, if my thoughts were correct, there had to be a reason for his behavior. What that reason could be, I was afraid to think about.

I admired the decor of the house on my way down to dinner. Much of it was Early American, and some of the furniture looked authentic, while other pieces appeared to be reproductions. There were also several modern pieces. I saw an Eames chair and ottoman in one of the rooms I passed, along with an elaborate stereo system. It was a warm, lived-in house with lots of paintings, books, and signs of Sara's presence, evidenced by an occasional toy haphazardly discarded in one or another of the rooms. I particularly admired the floors. Unlike the standard wall-to-wall carpeting seen everywhere in California, these floors were wide-planked of a lustrous, highly polished wood and covered here and there by lovely hand-hooked rugs. The house abounded in fireplaces—I even had one in my bedroom—but it wasn't air-conditioned, and the evening didn't feel noticeably cooler.

I met the others for a drink on the terrace before dinner and sat talking with Carol and her mother. Rick seemed to be pointedly ignoring me. Mrs. Allison suggested that Carol stay on in the house while I was there, rather than returning with them to town. The suggestion was ostensibly for Carol to keep me company, but I really think she had in mind that Carol would serve as a chaperon. I didn't feel I needed one but was happy to have her company.

Carol agreed, saying she'd follow her parents home after dinner and return with her clothes, and I offered to vacate her old bedroom.

"Oh, no, Katie, you keep it," she insisted. "I'm not nostalgic for my old room, and there are plenty of other bedrooms in the house. Actually, I think I'll take the one next to Sara's—she often has bad dreams at night, and I'll be able to go in and comfort her."

Again I wondered what damage my sister had wrought on her child that she suffered from bad dreams at such a tender age. But perhaps I was being unfair; Rick could be at fault as well.

Mrs. Gurney, the housekeeper, announced that dinner was ready, and we all went in to the dining room, a cheerful room with blue-and-white patterned wallpaper above white wainscoting and a large round table with ladderback chairs. There were touches of yellow in the seat cushions and vases of daisies were set on the buffet. I wondered if Susan had had a hand in the decorating or whether Mrs. Allison was responsible.

Sara stayed with us for dinner and sat on my left, the doctor seated on my right. We had meat loaf, potato salad, baked beans, and large glasses of iced tea, and there was little talk as we ate. I mentioned what a good cook Mrs. Gurney was, and Carol said she had been with them for years and that while she didn't live in, she was like part of the family.

At one point during the meal Sara spilled some baked beans on her dress and let out a cry, looking at me with stricken eyes rapidly filling with tears.

"It's all right, Sara," I said to her calmly. "It will wash out." But when I reached over to remove the beans from her lap, she shrank back as though expecting me to strike her. I looked up and saw that everyone's eyes were on me, but no one else said anything to Sara.

I put my hand over the child's small one. "Everyone has accidents, honey. I spill things all the time." I had been avoiding looking at Rick throughout the meal. Now I felt his eyes on me and, when I looked across the table at him, I saw he was thanking me with his eyes for my kindness to Sara. I was surprised that he thought being kind to a child was something requiring thanks.

We were served sherbet with our coffee, and while we sat over a second cup, Carol took Sara upstairs to put her to bed. The child had given me a lingering look before leaving the table, and I knew that the concept of twins was beyond her understanding and that, as far as she was concerned, I was her mother, albeit quite different from the one she was used to. And she wasn't ready to trust the differences.

"I'd like to discuss my sister's death now," I said to Rick when the child was out of earshot.

Before he could answer, his mother went into the kitchen to help Mrs. Gurney clean up, and Mr. Allison excused himself, saying he was going to take a walk to burn up some of the calories he had just consumed.

That left Rick and Dr. Sanders, and Rick suggested we all go into his study to talk privately.

The study turned out to be my very favorite room of all. It was square, not too large but perfectly proportioned. In front of French doors, open to a sweep of lawn and then the cliffs and ocean beyond, was a large writing table. It held an electric typewriter, stacks of paper, and a few books, and I gazed at it from a distance, intrigued by the idea that it was where Rick did his writing.

"What a lovely place to write," I murmured, looking around the room.

"Well, it's where I try to write. You notice I sit with my back to the view. If I didn't, I'd never get any work done."

The walls were paneled in dark wood, and built-in bookshelves covered most of the available wall space. I wanted to examine the book titles, but then wasn't the right time, so instead I seated myself in one of the comfortable leather arm chairs and took the snifter of brandy Rick handed me.

"I liked your last book," I said to him, and he seemed surprised that I had read it. Much longer than his previous books, it had traced a hundred years in the lives of a New England family. It could have been based on his own family, I suppose, but nothing in the book reviews had suggested that, and I didn't ask.

When we were all seated, Rick looked at Paul Sanders, who gave a little nod and then began speaking.

29

"An autopsy is being performed on your sister. We should know the exact cause of death sometime tomorrow. I must tell you, however, that I concur with Rick's feeling that it was probably suicide. Accidental death cannot be ruled out entirely, of course, but it would have had to be a freak accident for her to have gone off the cliff where she did."

I lifted my chin stubbornly at his arbitrary assumption that my sister was suicidal. "I don't accept the fact that my sister was capable of suicide. In fact, the letter I received from her today would clearly indicate otherwise."

I wasn't looking at Rick, so I don't know how he reacted to that statement, but the good doctor was clearly taken back. He obviously resented people questioning his diagnoses.

Rick's voice broke in to stop what might have become an argument between the doctor and me. "What did she say in the letter?"

"I'd rather you told me what happened." I was sorry for having mentioned the letter.

Rick gave me a long look. "It's understandable that you're upset, Kathryn. I'm sure you were very close to your sister, particularly since she was the only family you had. But it's been over five years since you've seen Susan, and she had changed quite a bit. For one thing, in the last few months she had become extremely erratic, which in part explains my daughter's behavior toward you, which I'm sure you noticed."

I looked at him defiantly, the brandy giving me courage. "Oh, yes, I noticed, and I'm perfectly willing to concede that Susan was probably not a good mother; I would have been surprised to learn otherwise. What *I'm* maintaining is that she was not capable of suicide."

30

Rick looked at Paul for help.

"Perhaps I can explain what Rick meant by her erratic behavior," he said to me, and I held out my glass to Rick for more brandy. "She would go from periods of listlessness to periods of frantic activity, from high spirits to depression."

"She was always like that," I interrupted him. There was a long silence while Paul and Rick exchanged looks.

"She was also indulging in—umm—uh—affairs," said the doctor in a hushed voice that I would normally have found laughable. He didn't look like the type to be shocked by affairs, and I thought he was overdoing it a bit.

"Affairs are hardly a reason for suicide," I pointed out to him. "Anyway, my sister never took men seriously." I realized as soon as I said it that it was hardly the thing to say in front of the grieving husband. I turned a stricken face to Rick.

"It's all right, Kathryn," he assured me. "I was well aware of that."

Paul's voice was serious. "Do you realize, Kathryn, that if, as you're suggesting, your sister did not take her own life, then it is probable that someone killed her?"

"Well, her letter—"

"Perhaps we should see this letter." Rick's voice indicated an unconcern he couldn't be feeling.

"I don't have it with me." I didn't add that it was safely upstairs in my purse.

"Perhaps you can tell us what it said," Paul suggested, his voice as seemingly disinterested as Rick's. But for some reason I didn't want to tell either of them what was in the letter.

"What about the newspapers? What did they say was the cause of death?"

Paul cleared his throat nervously. "Well, so far we've kept it out of the papers. We were hoping to get the results of the autopsy first. But I'm sure the wire services have picked it up by now. Rick is quite well-known, as you're aware, I'm sure, and we felt that adverse publicity—"

I stood up, almost too furious to speak, and glared down at Rick, my eyes narrowing. "I see. So it's to be hushed up because you're a famous writer and it might hurt the sales of your books, is that it? Well, let me tell you something, Mr. Allison. I think my sister was murdered. And I'll tell you something else. I'm not leaving this house until I find out who did it—with or without your help!"

Even in my fury I recognized that as a perfect exit line, and so, without waiting for a reply, I quickly left the room.

In the entry hall I met Carol, just leaving to pick up her things in town.

"You going to bed, Katie?" she asked me. "You're probably tired from your trip."

I glanced at the grandfather clock near the front door and saw that it was only nine-thirty.

"Good heavens, no. It's only six-thirty my time—I'd never get to sleep."

"Do you want to ride into town with me?"

I accepted her offer gratefully, not wanting to risk another encounter with Rick that night, and we quickly left.

We got back an hour later and met Paul as he was leaving the house.

"Kathryn, could I have a word with you?" he asked me.

I had cooled off by then, and when Carol suggested we use the screened porch in which to talk, I sat down with Paul and waited to hear what he had to say.

"Kathryn," he began, "I'm afraid you've gotten the

idea that there's some kind of a conspiracy here to make your sister's death appear to be a suicide."

Since that was exactly what I thought, I waited to hear what he would say next.

"Kathryn, Kathryn . . ." he said, sighing, his voice sounding very much like that of the old family doctor, which, considering his appearance, almost made me laugh. "Your sister was a very unhappy young woman. She had an unhappy marriage—"

"There are ways out of an unhappy marriage," I interrupted him, "other than suicide."

"But, Kathryn, if it wasn't suicide, as you're suggesting, then suspicion would naturally point to Rick. He's my oldest friend, Kathryn. I just couldn't believe that of him. And if you knew him as well as I do, you couldn't believe it either. I know he has a temper, and they quarreled a lot, but kill her? No, I just can't accept that."

"People do things in the heat of anger, Doctor."

"Paul. Call me Paul, please. No, forget about that, Kathryn. Put it right out of your mind. Your sister was a suicide 'type,' believe me. A doctor knows these things."

I stood up. "My sister was not a suicide type. My sister was a fighter—she never gave up. I don't think this conversation is getting us anywhere, Doctor, so I'll say good night."

I swept angrily past a startled Rick on my way into the house, and without a word to him, ran up the staircase and into my room. If the two of them thought I'd give up so easily, they were sadly mistaken. I was determined to stay in Cauley until I found out what had happened to Susan. Nothing they could do would stop me.

Chapter Four

I woke up the next morning, feeling hot and sticky, and opened my eyes to direct sunlight, which caused me to quickly roll over. I thought I must have overslept, but when I picked my watch up off the bedside table, I saw that it was only seven-thirty. It was rather a novelty to wake up to sunshine, but I would have preferred it without the oppressive heat. My cotton pajamas were sticking to my body, and even my hair felt damp.

I got out of bed and went to the window to look out. It was still and hot, the leaves hanging motionless on the trees, and the only sound was the crashing of the waves against the rocks far below out of my view.

I took a cold shower, then dressed in jeans and a T-shirt, making the bed before putting on my running shoes. I would have preferred going barefoot but was afraid my California ways might appear too casual to the household.

I didn't see anyone downstairs but smelled coffee and found Mrs. Gurney in the kitchen.

She looked around when I entered. "Breakfast won't be ready for half an hour yet," she informed me rather tersely, her tone less friendly than her appearance. She was a tiny, trim woman with soft gray curls framing a sweet-looking face.

34

I felt decidedly unwelcome and would have left the kitchen if I hadn't wanted some coffee so badly. "Could I get myself a cup of coffee?" I ventured, ready to retreat quickly if the answer was no.

She turned and looked at me again, this time pausing to study my face for a moment. "Of course, miss. How do you take it?"

"Just black, please."

She set the earthenware cup on a maple gateleg table, and I sat down and took a sip. It was delicious, much better than the instant I fixed myself at home.

The kitchen was cheerful and charming. The walls and appliances were white, and red-and-white checked curtains hung at the windows. A rocker with red corduroy cushions stood in a corner, and I imagined that Mrs. Gurney took well-deserved breaks in that chair.

"Is Sara up yet?" I inquired, thinking I'd take the child for a walk before breakfast.

"Mr. Allison drove her to nursery school. She goes every morning from eight to twelve."

"That must be fun for her, having other children to play with."

The housekeeper gave a restrained snort. "Don't know that she likes it all that well, but your sister liked to sleep in the morning."

I could hear the note of disapproval in her voice and realized she disliked me because of Susan. I felt like shouting, "I'm me, not my sister; I'm different!" But she probably wouldn't have believed it, and I knew I wouldn't be around long enough to change her mind about me.

I finished the coffee and rinsed the cup out in the sink, taking pleasure in Mrs. Gurney's look of surprise at my gesture.

"Can you tell me how to get down to the beach? I'd like to take a walk before breakfast."

She gave me a strange look, and I wondered how I could have been so stupid as to forget that that was where Susan's body had been found only the day before.

Her eyes avoided mine. "There're stairs cut out of the rock leading down," she murmured. "You'll see it at the end of the yard."

I thanked her for the coffee and went out the Dutch door that led to the terrace. I crossed the bricks, then walked through springy, damp grass until I came to the stairs she referred to. They were steep and winding and could have been dangerous if one fell against their jagged edges. But at the parts where the side was exposed to a sheer drop down the side of the cliff, there were sturdy guardrails. I paused when I came to the first one and looked down, wondering whether it was the spot where Susan had gone over. I could see that while a fall down the steps could be accidental, going over the side would have to be deliberate. But deliberate or not, it would be a terrible way to die, and I felt tears well up in my eyes at the thought of Susan falling to her death in such a way.

I continued down, surefooted in my running shoes, and it occurred to me that I hadn't been told who had found the body. I supposed it was Rick, but I made a mental note to ask him when I saw him, even though my question might antagonize him further. Even if he was innocent of any wrongdoing, and ended up hating me for my meddling, I had to find out who or what caused my sister's death. Not only because I felt compelled to find out what really happened, but because if I didn't make the effort, I didn't think anyone else would. I seemed to be the only one who cared.

I reached the bottom and sat down on the steps a moment to enjoy my first view of the Atlantic Ocean. It was wild and exciting, and I remembered Rick's comparing the Massachusetts coastline to that of Laguna Beach. I thought of my own view of the ocean in Seal Beach, where surfers came from miles around to ride the waves. Anyone foolish enough to try surfing here would soon be dashed against the massive rock formations.

The familiar smell of saltwater and the cries of the gulls pulled at my senses, and I got up to see if there would be enough of a beach for me to get in a little running before breakfast, knowing the exercise would offset the lethargy the heat seemed to be inducing in me.

The beach was only a narrow strip, broken up in parts by rocky promontories jutting out from the granite cliffs. It looked a likely spot for sunbathing, but not a safe place to swim. As for running, it would do. It wasn't, however, ideal. It was cooler down by the water, partly from the sea spray, but there was also a nice breeze coming in from the ocean.

I started to run to the south but hadn't gotten far when I spotted a young man, apparently asleep, his head and shoulders propped against one of the rocks. He had light-brown hair, curly and rather long. His body, clad only in bathing trunks, was muscular and deeply tanned.

I stopped short, not wanting to kick up sand on him as I ran by, and he opened his eyes and looked at me. His face quite literally turned white, despite his tan, and his eyes looked glazed with shock.

He flung an arm across his eyes and groaned. "Jesus, I'm hallucinating," I heard him mutter, and I realized he had mistaken me for Susan. I wondered who he was.

I was about to set him straight when he opened his eyes

and screamed at me in a voice filled with terror, "Go away! You're dead! Stay away from me."

It belatedly occurred to me that he could have killed my sister, and I turned and ran back to where the steps led up to the house. I didn't stop running until I arrived, breathless, on the terrace.

Rick and Carol were seated at a glass-topped table, breakfast set before them. Carol looked at me with some amusement.

"If you ran up all those stairs, you're in a lot better shape than I am. Sit down and have some breakfast."

Still gasping for breath, my side aching, I took a seat across from her. "Someone . . . on the beach . . . he . . . he . . . mistook me for . . . Susan," I managed to say. "But . . . he knew she was dead."

"Young? Curly brown hair?" she questioned me.

I nodded.

She and Rick exchanged glances. "Johnny Fowler," she said to him, and I saw his answering look.

"But he knew she was dead," I said insistently. "Maybe he—"

"Killed her?" Rick's tone was coolly disbelieving.

I looked at Carol. "But I thought it wasn't in the news yet. How would he know?"

She poured me a cup of coffee. "Several people know, of course. You can't keep something like that quiet. Johnny lives right next door."

"And he would be quite interested," murmured Rick.

Carol gave him a sidelong look. "Well, they *were* friends."

"They were lovers." He sounded bitter, and I felt uncomfortable hearing about Susan's indiscretions, particularly from her husband. But it was *my* sister who was

38

dead, and I wanted to find out why, so I didn't let the matter drop, as would be my normal inclination.

"Maybe they were just friends," I started to say, but Rick's contemptuous glance silenced me.

"Your sister was many things, Kathryn," he said, "but she wasn't devious. She conducted her affairs openly."

I felt myself blushing and tried to cover up my embarrassment by helping myself to bacon, eggs, and a toasted English muffin. It wasn't necessary, though, as Rick got up from the table abruptly and went into the house.

"He can't help being bitter, Katie, and with some justification."

I gave Carol a rueful look. "I know. I knew my sister, Carol, and I sympathize. But she didn't deserve to die so young—she just didn't!"

She reached over and covered my hand with hers. "You don't think it was suicide, do you?" she asked me.

I shook my head. "You knew her. What do *you* think?"

She was silent for a long time. "No, I can't see Susan killing herself, either. She wasn't the type."

It was good to hear someone agree with what I felt. I confess I was beginning to feel a bit paranoid about being the only one who thought it wasn't suicide.

"But if she didn't kill herself . . ." She left the sentence hanging in the air.

"I know. Someone else must have. I saw the guardrails —it couldn't have been an accident."

She looked distressed. "I know you think it was probably Rick, but there's no way I'd believe that."

"Why did she need affairs, Carol? What went wrong with her marriage?"

She looked surprised. "I don't think there was ever anything right about it."

39

I couldn't understand that. Surely they must have been in love in the beginning. "What do you mean?"

"Well," she seemed hesitant to answer me, "having to get married isn't—"

"You mean Susan was pregnant?"

"You didn't know?"

I shook my head. I thought back to that time when I was nursing my hurt and tried to remember if there had been any indications in Susan's behavior, but I could recall none. Perhaps if I had been more communicative with her, she might have opened up to me. No matter how I had acted, however, I knew realistically that she wouldn't have confided in me; she never did.

I could hear the phone ring in the house and then stop. Moments later Rick came out onto the terrace and spoke to me.

"The police chief just called. He's stopping by after lunch to give us the results of the autopsy. I thought you'd want to be here."

When he went back inside, Carol changed the subject. "Katie, I thought perhaps you'd like to go through your sister's things. She had tons of clothes, and there may be some things you'd like to have. Anything you don't want we'll give to the church for their rummage sale. And"— her eyes looked sad and she hesitated—"if you wouldn't mind, do you think you could pick something out for her to be buried in? Rick asked me to ask you—I really think he's at a loss about things like that."

"That's okay, Carol, I don't mind doing it." We were both beginning to get a little tearful and didn't say much as we had a second cup of coffee. Then Carol took me upstairs to my sister's room.

Rick and Susan had had separate bedrooms with a connecting bath. I didn't know whether to be dismayed by the fact or impressed. None of my married friends had separate bedrooms, or would even want them, for that matter. Nor, did I think, would I. I had always thought that one of the nicest things about marriage would be the closeness, the sharing. But I had seen magazine layouts of rich couples' homes where they had their own bedrooms, so perhaps it was a matter of having enough room and the means for such privacy.

Carol left to pick up Sara at nursery school, and I looked around the room with interest. It was different from the other rooms in the house, and I was sure she had done the decorating herself. It was all in beige and white, very subdued, elegant, and tastefully done. The doors, woodwork, and even the fireplace were painted white. Floor-length drapes in beige raw silk hung at the windows, and a matching silk spread covered the low modern bed of white lacquered wood. A chaise longue in creamy velvet was beside the fireplace, and a dressing table stood between the windows.

I opened the windows to let in some fresh air, then went over to the dressing table to admire the array of expensive perfume bottles. I had never seen so many in one place outside of a department store, and I tried a couple of them on my wrists. I remembered how Susan had always loved perfume, bubble bath, and anything that was scented sweetly, and I fought back tears that were threatening at this memory of her.

Next to the perfume a china cache box held a delicate gold watch from Cartier and a gold band that must have been her wedding ring. I thought perhaps she should be buried in the wedding ring and decided to ask Carol if that would be what Rick wanted. I set aside the watch, thinking Sara should have some of her mother's things when she was older.

I decided to go through the dressing table drawers and sat down on the bench. Aside from the reasons Carol had given me for going through my sister's things, I was also hoping to find something, some clue, that would help me discover how she had died. The right-hand drawer contained more jewelry—some gold chains that I set aside with the watch, several pairs of earrings, and one pair of diamond studs of a considerable size, all for pierced ears. That surprised me. So we weren't identical after all—I had never had my ears pierced.

The left-hand drawer was a clutter of hair rollers, side combs, countless lipsticks, and, at the bottom, a couple of color snapshots. I took them out. They had been taken at Christmas. A beautifully decorated tree stood in a corner of one of the pictures. One of them was of Rick and my sister and the other of Sara. Judging by Sara's size in the picture, they must have been taken the previous year. I looked more closely at the one of Susan and Rick. Something was wrong with it, but I couldn't put my finger on it. Then it came to me. Susan's hair was sun-streaked in the picture, just like mine was now. But either she was doing it artificially, or they must have gone south for some sun. She looked happy in the picture—happy and very lovely, and thinking back to my own lonely Christmas, I envied her that. I also set the pictures aside, hoping that Rick would let me take them home with me. I hadn't had a picture of Susan in years, and I would want to have some of Sara, too. The child was now my only relative.

Thinking about Susan looking so happy and also thinking about Sara being my only relative seemed suddenly too much, and I fell apart then, losing all of the control I had maintained since the news of Susan's death. I moved from the dressing table to the chaise lounge. Now that the tears had started I couldn't control them, and I flung myself on the lounge, my crying uncontrolled. I was remembering all the happy times I had spent with Susan when we were children, and was feeling very alone without her in the world anymore. I don't know how long I had been there when a hand clasped my shoulder.

I rolled over and faced the intruder. Rick stared down at me, his expression unfathomable. "I'm sorry . . ." I managed to say as he pulled me partly up to make room for himself, then pulled me against his chest.

"Go on, cry. You'll feel much better," he said to me in a voice that sounded slightly hoarse. He stroked my back and slid his fingers through my hair, murmuring to me all the while.

The surprise of finding myself in Rick's arms very soon put a stop to my tears. And, traitor that my body was, I was actually enjoying it to the point of trying to prolong my tears so that he wouldn't stop holding me. He must have sensed that I had somewhat recovered, though, because he suddenly held me away from him and brushed one sleeve gently across my face to dry the tears.

"What was it, Kathryn? Seeing her things?"

"I think—I think it was the pictures. The ones you took last Christmas."

He gave me a questioning look, and I pointed to where I had placed the pictures on the dressing table. He released me gently and got up, returning with the pictures.

He looked at them briefly, then turned to me. "What was it about them that made you cry?"

"You all looked so happy, and now Susan's dead. And I remembered how lonely I was last Christmas, and now

I'm the only one left, and I'll never have a family Christmas."

"Happy? Oh, maybe briefly while the presents were being opened. Your sister was rather acquisitive, but I'm sure you know that."

I drew away from him at that remark. She was only dead a day, and he couldn't say anything nice about her. I wondered if he ever had or whether the impression he made on me in California had been totally wrong, colored by my own young, romantic vision of what a famous author should be like. It had happened so long ago, and I could no longer be certain.

He took my hand, and I tried to draw it away, but he held fast to it. "Kathryn, do you expect me to be hypocritical about her just because she is dead? You seem like a nice young woman; my sister likes you, I know, and I've seen how you are with Sara. But you and your sister looked identical, and—"

"And so you thought we must have been alike in every way," I finished for him.

He gave me a measured look. "Identical twins usually are. I did research on the subject once for one of my books. Even twins who have been separated at birth have been found to have the same likes and dislikes, although their environments may have been totally different."

I would not be drawn into defending myself at the expense of my sister. And what was I to say, anyway? That it was different with us? I was the good twin, and Susan was the bad one? Nonsense! It was never a matter of good or bad; we were just different. While I sometimes, it is true, disapproved of what my sister did, she, on the other hand, believed me to be a complete ninny.

"I'm sorry she killed herself, Kathryn, I really am. I

44

won't pretend I loved her, but it was a waste—and completely unnecessary."

"She didn't kill herself," I said defiantly.

"You don't know what kind of state she was in. You weren't here."

"She didn't have the temperament to kill herself."

"She had threatened it before."

I moved as far away from him as possible on the chaise longue. "For what reason?"

He seemed hesitant to answer. "It was before we were married. She told me that if I didn't marry her, she would kill herself."

"Oh, that was just dramatics. Threats, yes. I'll believe that of her; she was always that way. But I don't believe that people who are always using suicide as a threat ever really do it. And I don't think you believe that, either."

He gave a harsh laugh. "And you think *I* killed her?"

"I think someone did."

He stood up then, looking down at me in anger. "I think you're the one given to dramatics, Kathryn. You may think what you wish, but please try not to disrupt my household while you're here." So saying, he turned and left the room, leaving me frustrated at not having had the last word, and at his having spoken to me as if I were a child.

I tried to think what I should do. I couldn't see Rick as a murderer, but I could see him and Susan, perhaps, having an argument on the stairs. Maybe she had been going to meet her lover, and he had tried to stop her, and she had fallen. Something like that could have happened. Not wanting a scandal attached to his name, Rick would try to cover it up by calling it suicide. And if that is what had happened, I would probably never find out the truth.

45

On the other hand, it was equally possible that someone killed Susan for a reason I didn't know about. If that were the case, perhaps I could do something to draw the person out—make him show his guilt. I was sure it was a he— Susan had never bothered enough with women to make them hate her.

I had hoped to find a clue in her room. If I didn't, and by then I didn't think I would, nothing would prevent me from saying I had, or even going so far as to produce one. It would have to be something in writing—a letter, a journal, a diary—something along those lines.

I heard Carol and Sara downstairs and looked at my watch. It was lunchtime, and I hadn't accomplished anything. After lunch, there would be the police chief; after that, I could get back to sorting out Susan's clothes.

Chapter Five

He didn't fit my preconceived notion of a police chief. He didn't look like one, act like one, or talk like one. Dr. Sanders, who had driven over with him, made the introductions, and when I held out my hand, he held it longer than was necessary, then gave a chuckle when I finally pulled it away in embarrassment. Tony Greco was a sexy man, and I wondered if he had ever met Susan.

Rick, Paul, Chief Greco, and I went into the study to hear the results of the autopsy. The chief took a seat behind the writing desk, Paul and I sat down, and Rick remained standing, leaning against the bookshelves.

Chief Greco produced some folded papers from his inside jacket pocket and spread them out on the desk in front of him. We waited while he appeared to be reading them. Finally Rick spoke.

"Cut the suspense, Tony, and let us hear the report."

The chief gave him a wry look. "Sit down, Rick. This will take a little time."

They seemed to know each other well, and I began to suspect that the whole thing might be rigged for my benefit. If Rick and the police chief were friends, the suicide theory would probably be accepted without question.

Rick gave a sigh of exasperation. "Come on, Tony. What was the cause of death?"

Tony Greco ran his fingers through his curly dark hair. "Even you can figure that out, Rick. The fall from the cliff killed her—her neck was broken, if you want the exact cause."

"I don't think she fell," I muttered, and Greco turned his gaze on me. I didn't say anything else. I was afraid of either crying over the heartlessness of their easy banter concerning my sister's death, or getting angry and saying something foolish. So I just stared back at him. He had the advantage, though, sitting with his back to the French doors. The light was shining in my eyes, and I couldn't see him as clearly as he could see me.

He reached into his pocket again and this time brought out a pair of glasses. He put them on, then picked up the autopsy report.

"Was your wife on any medication, Rick?"

Rick shook his head. "Not that I know of. Did you prescribe anything for her, Paul?"

Paul cleared his throat. "No. She asked me for diet pills once, but I told her I didn't believe in them."

"Susan was never fat," I said in protest to the doctor.

"She gained quite a bit of weight during her pregnancy. But she was able to take it off without the help of pills, as I knew she would."

I hadn't even thought of that. In fact, I had never considered how Susan must have looked when she was pregnant. Now that I did, I was sure she must have hated it, hated losing her figure, however briefly, for whatever reason.

Tony Greco's voice became serious. "The autopsy report gives the results of a toxicology test that was adminis-

48

tered. It's routine procedure, but the results it produced weren't routine. Large amounts of amphetamines and barbiturates were found in her blood."

"So that's why her behavior was so erratic," said Rick. "I should have guessed."

"We all should have guessed, but I should have been able to diagnose it," said Paul, sounding disgusted with himself. "I assumed, incorrectly it would seem, that her problem was mental, not physical."

"Did the drugs kill her?" I asked Tony Greco.

"No. As I told you, she died of a broken neck."

"Induced by too many drugs?" I persisted.

He took off his reading glasses and stared me down. "Induced by falling off the cliff."

"Well, where did she get the drugs?" I was determined to find out something helpful from him.

He shrugged. "Half the kids in town could have supplied her with them."

I thought of meeting Johnny Fowler on the beach that morning. He had clearly been on something at the time. Why else would he think he was hallucinating?

I locked eyes with Greco again. "Is there going to be an inquest?"

He gave Rick a questioning look.

"Kathryn thinks her sister was murdered," Rick told him, a touch of sarcasm in his voice.

"I gathered that, but why?"

"You'll have to ask her."

"Miss Wills," the chief addressed me formally, "there isn't going to be a coroner's inquest, because there is no evidence of foul play. Your sister, in a drugged state, either fell or jumped to her death. Absolutely no evidence to the contrary has been uncovered."

"Well, I uncovered some." I glanced around to see what reaction my statement had elicited. Rick looked as coolly unconcerned as ever. Paul stared at me in surprise. And the police chief chose that moment to blow his nose.

"It seems her sister wrote her a letter," Rick drawled.

"I have more than that," I said, improvising as I went along. "When I was going through her things this morning, I found a journal she kept."

"A journal?" Rick sounded surprised. "I bought her a journal once, but I didn't know she ever used it. I never saw her writing in it."

"Well, she did—quite extensively, in fact."

"Are you going to produce this journal, or were you planning to withhold evidence?" asked Tony Greco.

"I would like to speak to you alone," I told him.

"I'm her prime suspect, Tony," Rick informed him, his tone offhand. "She apparently isn't intelligent enough to consider that if I am a murderer, and she has some evidence, she's putting her own life in jeopardy."

The chief gave me a measured look. "All right, Miss Wills, we'll talk. Rick, Paul—would you mind—"

They left the room, and I moved to another chair where the sun wasn't in my eyes. "Chief Greco," I began.

"Call me Tony."

I didn't feel like calling him Tony, since I didn't consider his visit a social call, but I felt I had antagonized him enough. My feelings must have shown on my face, because he laughed.

"All right, call me whatever you want." His eyes half closed, he regarded me lazily, and for some reason I felt unnerved at being alone with him.

"How about dinner tonight?" If he was trying to disconcert me, he was succeeding.

"What?"

"You heard me. We can take a drive along the coast and find a seafood restaurant. You can tell me all about this mythical journal you found."

I glared at him.

"Did you think I had fallen for your story of a very convenient journal showing up? Rick was right, you know. If your sister has been murdered, you're opening yourself up to danger."

"That was the point."

"Why?"

"Because no one believes me. I know my sister didn't kill herself. And I don't think she could have fallen accidently, considering the way the guardrail is placed. And for the drugs, they were what are called uppers and downers, weren't they?"

He nodded.

"Well, I would hardly call using those being in a drugged state. She would know what she was doing."

"So?"

"Did you know my sister?"

He shook his head.

"We were twins—identical twins."

"I hope you're not going to give me some nonsense about ESP," he interjected.

"No, I'm not. But I'm telling you I knew her. She wasn't the type. She was a survivor."

He looked thoughtful. "She looked just like you?"

"Yes."

"It does seem strange, a beautiful young girl killing herself for no apparent reason."

"She wouldn't do it. I know she wouldn't."

"What about the letter. Was that real?"

51

"Yes. I have it with me upstairs. She said she was afraid and that Rick hated her."

"Anything else?"

"No."

"When you got it, did you take it seriously?"

"No," I admitted reluctantly. "Not at the time. I just thought she was being dramatic. The only thing is, she never wasted her dramatics on me because I knew her too well. She would have known I wouldn't take it seriously. Also, she hated writing letters."

"You might have a point, Kathryn."

"Miss Wills," I corrected him.

His eyes surveyed me at leisure until I felt myself flush.

"Is there anything else you want to tell me?"

I was about to say no when I remembered Johnny Fowler. I related the morning's incident to him.

"Why would Johnny want to kill her?"

"I heard they were having an affair."

"And?"

"Maybe she wanted to end it, and he didn't. Listen, young people take love very seriously. Maybe he thought he'd rather see her dead than with someone else."

He looked amused once again. "You're an authority on young people? You speak from your vast years of experience, no doubt."

"No, not vast years, but I teach in a high school, and I do know young people."

"Forgive me, Kathryn. I seem to enjoy baiting you."

I let his use of my first name pass. I wanted his help, after all, and he *was* exceedingly attractive. "Do you believe me, Tony?"

"I neither believe nor disbelieve. On the basis of what you've told me, I'm going to ask for a coroner's inquest.

I'll also start a thorough investigation. Will that satisfy you?"

I felt a great sense of relief to know that someone finally took me seriously, someone in a position to help. "Oh, yes. Thank you. Are you going to question Johnny Fowler?"

"Of course. I'll stop by there when I leave here."

I leaned back in the chair and smiled at him. A warm look came into his eyes.

"So how about dinner tonight?"

"No, not tonight. The funeral's tomorrow, and . . ."

He stood up. "All right, but I will want to keep you informed of what develops."

"Oh, yes."

"So perhaps another night."

I stood up and saw that our eyes were almost level. He was not much taller than me, thin but with more than a hint of strength in his muscular build.

"Yes, another night." I found myself looking forward to seeing him again.

He smiled. "Good. And, Kathryn—"

"You can call me Katie."

"Katie, be careful. No more wild stories about journals your sister kept. All right?"

"All right, Tony."

He took a step toward me, then seemed to hesitate. "I'll talk to you later. Take care."

53

Chapter Six

Tony left the house without saying good-bye to the others, and I went directly upstairs to finish going through Susan's belongings. It felt good to have an ally of sorts. I wasn't used to having my veracity questioned, but Rick and even Paul seemed to think I was like my sister, and they took nothing that I said seriously.

I must admit I was thinking of Tony as I went through Susan's clothes. I had nothing to wear if I did go out to dinner with him, and I decided it wouldn't hurt if I used some of them while I was there.

Sliding back the doors to her closet, I discovered a rainbow array of clothes that would have delighted me in other circumstances. Susan had never stinted when it came to clothes, and the closet, which revealed only her summer outfits, would have easily held every garment I had ever owned.

She had numerous silk pant outfits, dresses, and shirts, some in soft, subtle shades of beige and off-white, others in vivid turquoise, emerald, and fuchsia. I tried on a pair of pants and saw that our figures were still the same.

It was strange about Susan and me. Our figures were always identical, yet clothes tended to look different on her. I was slim and wore clothes well, but they seemed to mold to Susan's body sensuously, and the effect was startling. She moved her body differently than I did, with the sinuous grace of a cat, and if we walked down the street together, wearing exactly the same outfits, the eyes of men would follow her movements and completely ignore mine. Basically, I supposed, she had sex appeal, and I didn't, but since it seemed to be more an attitude than anything physical, I guessed I was stuck the way I was. Which is, of course, why Rick had treated me like a friendly older brother, while with Susan . . .

I made an effort to stop thinking about Rick. A dress in a light, foamy green struck my eye, and I pulled it out to try on. It was made of a soft cotton knit, as soft as a much-washed T-shirt, and the color brought out the green in my eyes and set off my tan. It was a wraparound style with slits up the sides, and it still had the price tag hanging from a sleeve. Because of that, I thought it would be all right to wear to dinner that night. Obviously Susan had never worn it. I also found a pair of white sandals with heels that I set aside to take to my room.

As I looked further through the closet, I found several more outfits with the price tags still on them, and I decided it would be silly of me not to make use of them while I was there.

The room was becoming unbearably warm, and the humidity seemed to be rising. I wanted to leave, perhaps go down to the beach for a swim, but I still needed to pick out clothes for Susan to be buried in.

I finally selected a lavender silk dress, delicate and lovely, and matching shoes. I left these items on the bed for someone to take to the funeral parlor, then, armed with the new clothes I was borrowing, including one of her bikinis, I went back to my room.

I hung up the clothes in my closet, then quickly got into the bikini. Grabbing a towel from the bathroom, I hurried down the stairs and out the door to the terrace.

Carol was seated there with Sara on her lap. The child's face lit up when she saw me.

"Go for a swim, Mommy?"

"That's your aunt Katie," Carol corrected her. Sara gave a smug smile. I think she understood I wasn't really her mother, but she just didn't want to admit it.

"The humidity really bothers me," I told Carol. "How do you stand it?"

"Not too well." She laughed. "But it feels like it's going to rain soon. That ought to help."

"I'm going for a swim. Do you want to come along?"

She wrinkled her nose. "I'm too lazy to move."

"Can I go with you?" Sara tugged at my heart, she seemed so in need of a mother's love. I looked at Carol who shrugged.

"Take her down with you if you want. She's a good child—she'll play in the sand while you swim."

I held out my hand, and Sara was beside me in a flash, her warm, sticky hand enclosed in mine. I led her slowly down the steps to the beach, listening to her chatter about nursery school. I'd never been around little children, only those of high school age, and it was a novelty.

It wasn't discernably cooler by the ocean, although there was a slight hot breeze off the water. I let go of Sara's hand and waded in up to my knees. The water felt icy, much colder than the Pacific, but that was partly because the air was so hot. Sara was wearing shorts and a halter top, and I didn't think anyone would mind if she got wet, so I removed her socks and sneakers, leaving them next to the towel, then led her into the water with me.

She seemed frightened at first, but soon she was splashing around while I sat at the edge and let the waves roll over my legs and the spray cool off my body. I didn't hear anyone approaching. My first indication that we weren't alone was when I saw Sara look wide-eyed at something behind me, and then I turned around.

Johnny Fowler, dressed in cutoff jeans, gave me a rueful grin.

"Sorry about this morning—I hope I didn't scare the hell out of you." He sat down beside me in the wet sand.

"Not at all. I thought it was the other way around."

"Yeah—I thought I was seeing a ghost. You sure look alike."

"Identical twins usually do."

"Well, anyway, I wanted to apologize."

I gazed at him thoughtfully. He seemed disarmingly young and friendly, and it took an effort to see him as my sister's lover. When I had known her, she preferred older men.

"How did you know she was dead?" It wasn't the smartest question to ask if he had killed her, but I couldn't really picture him as a murderer. I had trouble picturing *anyone* as a murderer.

"Yeah, well, I wanted to explain about that. The local fuzz was at our house awhile ago, and I leveled with him. You see, I saw her—yesterday morning on the beach— and she was dead. I mean, I checked on that. I wouldn't have just left her there to die. But then I panicked and ran—I was afraid someone would think *I* did it. Anyway, I'm sorry. Honest."

"You were afraid someone would think you did what? You mean you don't think she killed herself, either?"

"Susan? Hell, no! She enjoyed life. Why would she kill herself?"

"Did you tell Chief Greco that?"

"Yeah, but I'm sorry I did. I think it put me on his list of suspects."

Sara came over and sat down between my legs, leaning back against me.

"Did he tell you about the autopsy report?" I asked him.

"You mean about the drugs?"

"Yes."

"Yeah, he told me. What's the big deal? Everyone takes them."

I looked him in the eyes. "Were you supplying her?"

I would swear his look of surprise was genuine. "Are you crazy? She was supplying me. And half the other kids in town."

I considered that for a moment and was saddened to realize I could believe it all too easily. "Did you tell Greco that?"

"No way."

"Why not?"

"Well, it's not exactly legal, you know. You going to tell him?"

I gave him a level look. "Not if you'll help me."

"A little coercion, huh?"

"You could call it that."

He laughed. "I like you. You have a sense of humor. Susan didn't."

"Susan obviously had other attributes you liked."

"Listen, I wasn't having an affair with your sister, if that's what you're thinking. I know there was talk because we were seen together a lot, and she also said her husband

58

suspected us of carrying on. But I swear, we never made it. We got high together once in awhile—used to meet right here, as a matter of fact—but other than that it was strictly business."

I don't know why, but I believed him. I just couldn't see Susan getting interested in such a nice kid. "Where was Susan getting the stuff?"

"Hell, I don't know that. It's not smart to reveal your source."

I sighed with disappointment. "Well, can you tell me who else she was supplying?"

"Listen—hey, what's your name, anyway?"

"Katie."

"Listen, Katie, we're not talking about heroin and junkies and all that stuff. Nobody kills for some bennies. I mean, that would be like killing for a joint. No way. She was killed for some other reason, and I'd put my money on the jealous husband."

"Rick?"

"Yeah. Hey, I like Rick, you know, but I'd say he had just cause. Your sister really got around."

"I like my idea better."

"Yeah? Well your idea won't wash. Sorry."

"Do you know who she was having an affair with?"

"No, she never talked about it. I do know she was really uptight about something the past couple of weeks. But she didn't say anything to me about it, and I didn't ask. Now I wish I had."

Clouds were moving in overhead, making the sky darken. Only tiny patches of blue could still be seen and soon even those disappeared. As I watched I saw a streak of lightning flash through the sky, followed by a crash of thunder.

Sara gave a shriek, and I put my arms around her and held her close, watching the sky in fascination. California doesn't get thunderstorms, and I found the whole thing exciting.

Johnny excused himself. "Listen, Katie, if you want to know anything else, just give me a call. Okay?"

I nodded, and he took off down the beach toward his house.

Sara was wriggling in my arms. "Are you scared, Sara?" I asked her.

She turned an impish face up to me. "Little bit."

Then the rain came down hard. It felt marvelously cool and refreshing after the oppressive heat. I stood and picked up Sara. Feeling like a modern-day druid, I danced around with her on the beach, the rain so heavy, it practically obscured my vision. Somehow the rain seemed to bring out my energy, which had lain dormant in the humidity.

Sara didn't want to be held, so I put her down, and we did a rain dance together, both of us laughing out loud in delight.

"Uncle Paul," I heard Sara cry out, and turned to see the doctor, clothes plastered against him from the rain, coming down the stairs.

He lifted Sara up and set her on his shoulders. "Carol thought you might need rescuing," he said to me with a grin.

"Oh, we're all right. We were in bathing suits anyway. But look at you—you're soaked."

"Don't worry about me. I'll put on something of Rick's. Anyway, I wanted a chance to talk with you alone."

He looked very appealing with the water dripping off

him. "Sorry about last night, Paul. I'm afraid I was rather rude to you."

"Hell, Kathryn, I came down here to apologize to you. I guess you know the results of the autopsy changed my thinking. If I could be wrong about her mental condition, then I could be wrong about a lot of other things, too. Not that I'm ruling out suicide, mind you, but I'm going to try to keep an open mind. Lucky you found that journal— that should tell Tony Greco a few things, I should imagine."

I gave him a sheepish grin. "Oh, I just made that up about finding a journal. I thought it would make the police take me seriously, but Tony saw through it right away."

He smiled at that. "Tony's a good cop, Kathryn; you ought to just let him do his job."

"Has anyone ever told you, Paul, that you tend to be bossy?"

"All the time. And at the risk of appearing bossy once again, could I suggest we get in out of the rain? I, for one, could use a drink."

Carol and Rick were standing under the covered part of the terrace when we got back up, and Rick looked relieved to see us. His eyes went from Paul to me before raking my body in the scant bathing suit with a look of distaste. I wondered what he had expected me to go swimming in. At home I practically lived in a bikini during the summer, but perhaps New Englanders weren't as casual.

Carol grabbed hold of Sara, who was continuing to dance on the terrace. "I'll get her ready for dinner while you change," she told me, and I followed her into the house and up the stairs.

One glance into my room was enough to tell me that someone had searched it with a vengeance. I felt shaken, as though a private part of me had been violated. And then I felt anger, outrage, and turned and went back downstairs to confront Rick with the news. I found him at work in his study.

When I appeared in my bathing suit, he gave me a disapproving look. "You wanted something, Kathryn?"

"Someone searched my room," I said to him, hoping to wipe the supercilious look off his face.

But he just looked annoyed. Nonetheless, he followed me back upstairs to my room, looking around it in silence for a moment before turning to me.

"Was anything taken?"

"I haven't looked, but what would anyone want?"

"Perhaps the murderer was after that incriminating journal you found," he said dryly.

He certainly had the facility for making me angry. "Look, Rick, this happened in *your* house. It's *your* responsibility. I don't find it amusing."

He frowned. "Sorry. You're quite right. Do you want me to phone the police?"

"Why is it *my* decision? It's your house that was broken into—unless, of course, you did it yourself."

"What do you want from me, Kathryn?" He sounded tired, as though I was taxing his strength.

I felt defeated by his indifference. "Nothing, Rick. I don't want anything from you. My sister was killed, and you couldn't care less, although she was your wife and the mother of your child. Someone searched my room, and if he didn't find what he wanted, he will probably search it again. But don't worry your head about any of it, Rick. Just go on as though nothing's happened. And please make my excuses at dinner; I've found I've lost my appetite. And, Rick, one more thing before you go. I won't be returning to California tomorrow after the funeral. I'll move out of your house, because I know I'm not welcome, but I'll take a room in town. I'm staying here until I find out what really happened to Susan, and nothing you do will stop me."

I wanted to get some reaction out of him—anger, concern, anything. If he couldn't comfort me, at least I thought he could yell at me. But all he said before turning to leave was, "I'll have Mrs. Gurney bring a tray up to you."

Chapter Seven

I straightened up the room, not caring if I destroyed evidence. I knew there would be nothing missing, and there wasn't. Even Susan's letter was still in my purse, but its contents wouldn't have incriminated anyone.

It gave me an uncomfortable feeling, though, to know that someone's hands had touched my belongings, and I began to understand why people got upset over things like invasion of privacy. It also bothered me to note that there wasn't a lock on my bedroom door. Not that I had *ever* had a bedroom door that locked, but now I wanted one.

I took a shower, then dressed in my pajamas. It was still pouring outside, and the temperature had dropped considerably. I couldn't think of anything else to do, so I got into bed. I didn't even have anything to read and wished I hadn't been so hasty in declining dinner with the others.

About an hour later there was a knock on the door. It was Carol, and I told her to come in. She was carrying a dinner tray and put it down beside me on the bed.

"Listen, Katie, I was wondering if you had picked anything out for Susan. Paul's driving back to town now, and he offered to drop the clothes off at the funeral home."

"Yes, I put them out on her bed."

"Thanks. I know Rick will appreciate it."

"Rick doesn't appreciate anything I do," I said sarcastically and immediately was sorry. I knew I shouldn't take my bad temper out on my one friend.

"I don't think you understand something, Katie. Whenever Rick looks at you, he sees Susan. I don't think he understands you're a different person. It's as though you're a continuation of her."

"That's ridiculous."

"Not really. I instinctively liked you when we met, which didn't happen with your sister. But I really don't think Rick sees the differences. And you do seem to be giving him a hard time."

"Well, he deserves it. Anyway, I like you, too. Why don't you sit down and talk to me while I eat?"

"I have to take the clothes down to Paul. He wants to get started back before the roads flood. I'll come up later."

I was looking over the food without much enthusiasm when another knock came at the door. It opened, and a small head peered around it. "You can come in, Sara," I told her.

She came in and stood just inside the door, smiling tentatively at me. She looked adorable in pink cotton pajamas with ruffles.

"Will you tuck me in?" She asked the question tentatively, as though she half expected to be refused.

"I'd love to tuck you in," I assured her, and it was true. I wished Susan had told me I had a niece, had let me meet her. Despite Rick's attitude, I vowed to keep in touch with Sara after my return to California.

I put on my robe and followed her down the hall to her room. It was just an ordinary bedroom. Except for a few toys scattered around, I would have taken it for a guest room. If she were my child, I would have put up some wallpaper with pictures of nursery rhymes and painted the furniture white.

She climbed into her twin bed, and I tucked a blanket around her. I was glad it was cool enough for one, the previous night having been so miserably warm.

"You get book?" she asked me, nestling down under the covers.

"What book, Sara? You want me to read you a story?"

"No, your book. You get it?"

"What book are you talking about, honey?"

She sat up in bed and frowned at me, and I tried not to laugh at her serious little face.

"Under there," she said, pointing down along the side of the bed.

I knelt down on the floor and looked under the bed, but there was no book.

"No, no. Not there." She seemed to be getting excited, and I wished I could find the book for her.

She jumped out of bed, then reached under the mattress and pulled out a slim book, something like a ledger.

"Here's your book, Mommy. Did you forget it?"

I tucked her in again, then sat down next to her on the bed and opened the book. It was, indeed, some sort of a ledger book with amounts of money after a long list of names. I was sure it was important but wanted to wait until I got back to my room to look at it more closely.

"Do you want me to read you a story, Sara?"

"Yes, please."

I looked around the room for a book to read to her and finally found one about a naughty bear, that she seemed to enjoy. At the end she was practically asleep, and I bent over and gave her a good-night kiss, feeling gratified when her arms went around my neck and she gave me a hug.

66

I stayed a few moments longer until she fell asleep, then got up to go.

Rick was standing in the doorway, watching me, a look of uncertainty on his face. He was dressed in light-blue denim pants and a matching shirt, a lock of his hair falling across his forehead. He looked boyish and vulnerable, and for a moment I felt as tender toward him as I did for Sara.

He walked over to the side of the bed and looked down at Sara as I tucked the ledger book between the folds of my robe.

"She's a precious child. You're very lucky," I said to him softly, not wanting to awaken Sara.

He transferred his gaze to me. "Yes, I have been very lucky with *Sara,*" he said, stressing the name Sara very slightly.

I got up, and we both walked to the door. I was pressing my hand against where the book rested beneath my robe, hoping it wouldn't fall to the floor.

"Kathryn, I think we should talk."

I looked down at my attire, thinking it not quite suitable for a private talk with him.

"You're fine the way you are."

Although I knew I was more fully covered than I had been in the bathing suit, I didn't really feel in control wearing pajamas and a robe. Anyway, it was only a little after eight o'clock. I thought I'd like to get dressed and join the others for the rest of the evening.

"No, let me put some clothes on, Rick. I'll come downstairs in a few minutes."

In my room, I slid the ledger book between my mattress and box spring. I didn't think it was the best hiding place, but I also didn't think my room would be searched again that evening, since it had been so thoroughly searched earlier. I didn't want it to remain in Sara's room, although it might have been the safest place. The child might let something slip about the book, and I didn't want her placed in any danger whatsoever.

I was loathe to put on my jeans and T-shirt again, as they were badly in need of a wash, so I dressed in the green dress I had taken from Susan's closet, and also the white sandals. I combed my hair, put on a little lip gloss, and went downstairs to find Rick.

I found Rick and Carol in the living room, a pleasant room dominated by an enormous red-brick fireplace and cheerful chintz-covered furniture in a flowered pattern. Carol was curled up in a chair, reading a book, and he was standing looking out at the rain, a glass in his hand.

"Would you care for a drink, Kathryn? A little brandy, perhaps?"

I accepted the brandy, hoping it wouldn't go to my head after having eaten virtually none of the dinner that had been brought up to me. The air was chill now with a dampness to it, and I found the drink warming. We sat down on the couches that faced each other in front of the fireplace, and I waited for him to speak.

He leaned back on the couch, his legs crossed, and lighted a cigarette. "Carol and Paul gave me quite a talking-to at dinner tonight. It seems I've been treating you quite badly. Carol, for one, told me that if you left this house tomorrow, she was going with you, and Paul intimated that my hospitality left a lot to be desired."

I glanced over at Carol and saw her grinning into her book. I stifled a smile.

"Anyway, please feel at home here as long as you wish to remain. Even without the opinions of Paul and Carol,

I can see how much Sara likes you, and I think you're good for her."

The brandy was making me feel more at ease with him than I usually did. "Thank you, Rick. I really can't stay too long, but I hate to leave before I find out what really happened. I know you don't believe that anything did, but—"

"That's another thing we discussed at dinner, and we all came to the conclusion that you are probably right and we had been too ready to believe it was suicide. You see, Kathryn, your sister's behavior had been extremely erratic lately, and Paul and I were watching the symptoms closely, fearing she was on the verge of a breakdown. Of course, the autopsy report destroyed that theory in a hurry. Paul no longer seems to think it was suicide, nor does Carol, but, quite honestly, Kathryn, none of us could think of anyone who would have killed her. It wasn't that your sister was universally loved—quite a few people disliked her—but no one disliked her enough to kill her. And I wish I could make you believe that if I had wanted to get rid of Susan, I would simply have divorced her. It was coming to that, anyway."

"The jealous husband is always the prime suspect," came Carol's voice from across the room, and I had to nod in agreement.

"Carol, little sister," he said to her in an exasperated tone, "come over *here* and say that."

Carol flopped down on the couch next to me and grinned at him. "Well, it's true, Rick."

"And did you think I was jealous?"

"Well, no. It didn't seem to me you cared enough to be jealous. But if she was making you look ridiculous, well
—"

"You think I would kill her for *that?*"

"Not really. But I often wondered why you didn't divorce her."

"Because I would have lost Sara."

"Well—there's your motive!"

"Listen, Carol, you're joking around, but Kathryn is sitting there, taking you quite seriously."

I shook my head at him slowly. "No, Rick, I can't see you as a cold-blooded killer. But I knew my sister. I know how infuriating she could be, and perhaps if you were quarreling, you might have struck out at her."

"And shoved her off the cliff?"

"I could see it happening that way. And if it *was* an accident, Rick, I would understand."

He got up from the couch and paced around the room, finally stopping at a table where he refilled his glass from a decanter and drank it down in what seemed like one gulp.

"Yes, you're right," he said at last. "It could have happened that way. But it didn't."

"Look," I said to him, "I'm having trouble seeing *anyone* I've met here as a killer. But quite aside from Susan's death, someone did search my room, and I take that very seriously, even though you don't seem to."

"Yes, I got hell from everyone about that, too. I thought perhaps *you* had done it just to stir up trouble."

"Katie wouldn't do that," said my ally.

"Yes, Carol, but if Kathryn didn't do it, that leaves Paul or myself. We were the only ones who knew about the journal she found among her sister's effects."

Carol turned to me in surprise. "What journal? I didn't know about any journal."

I hated to lie to Carol and couldn't see any point in

keeping up the pretense about the journal, particularly since I had now found something that was probably much more important than a journal. "There wasn't a journal, Carol. I made that up to . . . well, to flush out the killer."

She gave me an astonished look. "That was insane! Your room was searched, and you could be in danger."

"I know—it was stupid of me. But I wanted Tony Greco to take me seriously. And he did, actually, but not because of a journal; he knew I was making that up from the start."

Rick sat down again. "What about the letter? Was that real?"

"Oh, yes. I got that in the mail right before you called me. But all it said was that she was afraid. And that you hated her. But they didn't seem to be connected—she didn't say she was afraid of you. It was more like she was afraid but couldn't depend on you for protection, since you hated her."

"Yes, my wife did tend to be overly dramatic. I probably wouldn't have taken her seriously if she had told me she was afraid, particularly since I thought she was becoming mentally unbalanced."

I nodded my agreement. "Yes, I know what you mean. I didn't take her letter seriously when I got it. But, of course, now—"

Carol looked from Rick to me. "So, what do we do now? If someone killed her, we can't just ignore it, but putting your own life in danger is very foolish, Katie."

"What did Tony say, Kathryn?"

"He said he'd investigate."

"Then I think we should leave it in his hands. He is very capable, Kathryn, and the police force in town is excellent."

71

"If inexperienced," Carol muttered.

"Well, no, they don't have much experience with crime, but Tony's excellent, and if it *is* drug-related, they do have experience with that."

"Incidentally," I told them, "Susan wasn't having an affair with Johnny."

"How do you know that?" asked Carol.

"He told me, and I believe him."

"No—I wouldn't have thought he was her type," said Carol.

Rick didn't look convinced. "She was with him a lot, I know that. And she told me on several occasions that she got from him what she couldn't get from me." He looked a bit embarrassed at this admission, and I could just hear my sister taunting him with words to that effect.

Johnny had asked me not to mention the drugs, and I saw no reason to at this time. But I thought Carol and Rick were both intelligent enough to put two and two together for themselves.

Carol looked at her watch. "There's a movie coming on I want to watch, if you'll excuse me."

I didn't think I could concentrate on a movie, and Rick seemed disinclined to leave, so we stayed where we were.

"About Sara, Rick. She really seems confused about who I am. Isn't it going to be difficult to explain when I leave?"

"Of course it is. I hadn't even gotten around to explaining where her mother was, and then you appeared. I think she wants to believe you're her mother but can't quite understand why you're suddenly acting differently with her. I suppose I'll just have to tell her when you leave that her mother's gone away, and wait until she's older to tell her the real facts. Although it won't make much difference

72

whether her mother killed herself or was killed; either one will be awfully hard for a kid to take."

It was a mess, and I didn't envy him the responsibility. "Who will take care of her now?"

"Mrs. Gurney and myself, the same as always. Your sister seldom took the role of motherhood seriously. Don't worry about it. She'll be all right."

He asked if I'd like a refill on the brandy, and I held out my snifter. I was feeling very relaxed and almost at home.

"I hope you'll let me see Sara and keep in touch with her as she grows up. She's my only relative, you know, and I've grown to love her already. Unless you think my looking like her mother would be too confusing for her."

"We'll work something out." He lighted another cigarette and looked at me through the smoke. "You look lovely in that dress, Kathryn."

I flushed from the compliment, which was so unexpected, and from the knowledge that I was wearing one of his wife's dresses without his permission.

"It belonged to Susan; I hope you don't mind. Carol said it would be all right. I didn't bring much with me."

He seemed to ignore my nervous babbling. "You seem soft and sweet and quite . . . desirable."

"You were certainly generous with her," I said in an attempt to change the subject. "I've never seen such a wardrobe. Your books must have done very well." It wasn't the most tactful of remarks. How well his books were doing was hardly any of my business.

He seemed to bestir himself on the couch. "What are you talking about?"

"Susan's wardrobe—I've never seen anything like it. This still had the price tag on it, and it would have cost me more than a week's salary. Her whole closet is filled with designer clothes. I was really impressed. You certainly seemed to be good to her as far as money went."

"I'm not quite following you, Kathryn. My wife spent very little on clothes. She had charge accounts, but what she spent never added up to much. She was just a careful shopper and probably bought things on sale."

I should have dropped the subject there. It was none of my business what his wife spent on clothes. But it occurred to me that Susan had acquired a lot of money from somewhere, and maybe it was important to find out where. "Look, Rick, take my word for it. Susan has several thousands of dollars worth of clothes upstairs in that closet. And if *you* didn't pay for them, I'm wondering where she got the money."

"I think you must be mistaken."

He was making me angry again, but I couldn't let go of it. "I am not mistaken, Rick. As usual, you assume I don't know anything. Well, I know designer labels when I see them, and I'm also capable of reading price tags. So forget it—keep hiding your head in the sand, if that makes you happy. But I think I'll mention it to Tony Greco. He, at least, doesn't treat me like a backward child!" I got up to leave, but he caught me by the door, taking hold of my arm and swinging me around toward him.

"Do you always lose your temper so easily, Kathryn?" His voice was amused, and his eyes mocked me.

"No, only with you," I retorted, and was about to say more when he pulled me to him and, reaching down, covered my mouth with his. At first I fought him, but that only made him pull me more closely to him, and then I found that I really didn't want to fight him at all. It was like one of the many daydreams I had had about him coming true at last, and I wound my arms around his neck

74

and pressed myself even closer to him, wanting it never to end.

As I pulled closer to him, I felt him tense, then pull away from me, holding me at arm's length as though it had been I who had made the advance.

His voice was a soft caress. "No, you're not identical. Not at all."

"Rick," I began, moving toward him again, feeling vulnerable and suddenly shy.

"I'm sorry, Kathryn—I shouldn't have done that." A closed look came over his face, and I felt shut out. Suddenly close to tears, and not wanting him to see the effect he had on me, I broke away from him and ran upstairs, taking refuge once more in my room.

I flung myself across the bed, letting the tears flow. I thought about his kiss. Either he had kissed me because I reminded him of Susan and he still desired her, or he had kissed me . . . well, I really couldn't think of any alternative. He didn't know me well enough yet to be attracted to me. It had to be Susan. I would always remind him of her, and that would be disastrous. Either I would be a substitute for her, a constant reminder to him of his lost love, which I wouldn't be able to bear, or he would love me for myself, but I would be a constant reminder to him of the woman he had hated. It would be in my own best interests to forget all about Rick, finish my business as quickly as possible, and get back home to California and put three thousand miles between us.

But I couldn't help thinking how nice it would have been if he had married me instead of her. I loved it here— loved his house, his sister, his daughter. I loved the books he wrote and would have been so proud to be married to him. But he had made his choice, and it was too late to go back now.

The rain had not let up at all. It lashed against the windows with a force that made them rattle, and I could hear the crashing of the waves against the rocks. All alone, in the dark, in a room that had been violated only hours before, I began to be afraid, and I couldn't get it out of my mind that it would be so easy for someone to break into the house, under cover of the storm, and kill me as I lay sleeping.

Once I had expressed the thought in my mind, I couldn't seem to get rid of it. I got off the bed and went over to the windows to make certain they were locked. As I looked down at the terrace I thought I saw a dark shape moving down on the ground, but in the next instant it was gone, and I chided myself for imagining things. I made sure the windows were latched, then went into the bathroom and locked that window, also.

Of course I knew the old "chair under the doorknob" trick, and while I hated the thought that someone might, by forcing the door, break the dainty little antique chair I wedged underneath the knob, I did it nonetheless. My life was more important than a chair.

I took comfort from the fact that there was an extension phone on the table next to my bed. If someone did try to break in, I could at least call the police. I picked it up to listen to the reassuring dial tone, but it was dead. After a moment of panic, I realized that the storm had probably knocked down some power lines. Anyway, it would take too long for the police to arrive—I would be much better off simply screaming and alerting the household to the danger.

Then I remembered the ledger book and got it out from

beneath the mattress. When I opened it, the first thing that struck me was that it wasn't in Susan's handwriting. I didn't know why I hadn't noticed that before, except that I had only glanced at it briefly and had just assumed that it was something she had kept. The writing wasn't very legible, and I couldn't decipher the names, but I thought that someone familiar with any of them would be able to. The amounts of money, however, were very easy to read, and I decided that whatever sort of business it was, it certainly was lucrative. If it wasn't in Susan's writing, I couldn't understand what she was doing with it. Perhaps she had stolen it, I speculated, and whomever it belonged to had killed her because of it. I thought it most probably belonged to the person supplying Susan with the pills, and I could understand that he wouldn't want her to know his business. But if he knew she had it, and had killed her for it, he probably wouldn't hesitate to kill again. And since I had it, I decided to turn it over to Tony Greco the first chance I got the next day. Perhaps he'd invite me out to dinner again. He was a most attractive man, and my day-dreams about Rick were futile.

I'm not usually a nervous person, but that night my mind wouldn't seem to stop concocting new dangers that I was in, and most of the night I tossed around in the bed, making a shambles of the sheets and wishing I had one of Susan's pills to help me sleep.

When I did finally sleep, my dreams were terrifying nightmares of being pushed over a cliff with no one coming to my aid. And yet, even in my dreams, I had no idea who the enemy was.

Chapter Eight

The funeral was an ordeal. I felt as if I was on stage, the center of attention, the audience watching my every move.

The chapel was crowded, most of the people presumably friends of Rick and his family, and when I walked in with Carol and Paul, Rick having gone on ahead, every eye was on me. I could see that the news of my presence, or even my existence, hadn't circulated, and it was all I could do to maintain my composure in the face of such curiosity.

There was a hushed silence when I viewed the body. Several tactless people actually followed me to the front of the church to make comparisons. Susan looked at peace, and I couldn't seem to tear my eyes away from that last glimpse of her. Carol put her arm around me and glared at some of the onlookers, then led me back to my seat.

I found my mind wandering during the minister's eulogy. He meant well, I suppose, but he obviously hadn't known my sister, and who he was describing seemed more like an angel on high who had briefly visited us and made the earth a better place for having been here. Susan would have laughed if she had heard it. I finally tuned him out, and instead I concentrated on my own memories of her and found that there were many good ones. When our parents had been killed, she had sat by my bed night after night, lulling me back to sleep after my bad dreams had made me cry out and awaken her. She had had great strength during that time, and I had relied on her completely.

I was hardly aware of the tears streaming down my face until Paul, who was seated beside me, handed me his handkerchief and turned a concerned face toward me.

Carol, Rick, and their parents drove to the cemetery in the limousine, and I elected to drive with Paul. He remarked that I had caused quite a sensation in the chapel, but not to take it personally. It was only natural that people would be taken back when they saw the exact likeness of the one they had come to see buried. I told him that I understood, but it embarrassed me to be stared at so openly.

The cemetery was lovely—old and quaint and set behind a typical New England church. Carol told me that several generations of their family had been buried there, and I was glad Susan would be in such a peaceful place.

The rain had stopped sometime during the night or early morning, and it was a perfect day. A cool breeze off the ocean kept it from being too warm.

Tony Greco was at the cemetery. I caught his eye and tried to tell him with mine that I needed to speak to him. He nodded, and I think he understood.

When the graveside ceremony was over, several people came up to Rick to express their condolences, and I was introduced to some of his friends. I noticed a man staring at me. He wasn't the only one, of course, but his stare was of such an intensity, and he was looking at me with such familiarity that for a moment I thought I must know him.

But I was sure we had never met, because if we had, I didn't see how I could have possibly forgotten him.

He was large, several inches over six feet, with tremendous shoulders and arms. He had a head of flaming red hair and a full beard to match. He put me in mind of a huge, cuddly teddy bear, although I'm sure he would have hated the description. When he saw that he had captured my attention, he took several giant steps over to me, then stood there, looking at me with a beaming face. I couldn't help it—I had to smile back at him, such was the force of his good humor.

"You're Kathryn, aren't you? I was hoping you'd come."

I couldn't believe I had actually heard him correctly. It seemed incredible that someone here had prior knowledge of my existence.

I reached out my hand, and he took it, quite swallowed it up in his own, in fact. "Yes, I'm Kathryn. Did you really know about me?"

"Of course. Susan talked about you often. Oh, I'm so glad to see you here, I was afraid you wouldn't come, that you'd stay in California."

He finally let go of my hand but still stood there smiling at me.

"You know who I am, but—" I began, and he laughed a deep, hearty laugh that caused several people to look around in shock.

"I'm Mike Campbell. Sorry, my ego is such that I'm absolutely convinced everyone in the world has heard of me."

I smiled at him. "Don't worry about it—it takes a while for news to reach the coast."

He grabbed my hand then and led me out of earshot of the others.

"Kathryn, love, we must get together. I have so much to tell you, but this isn't the place. How about it, will you come see me tomorrow?"

The "so much to tell you" interested me, of course, and I was again having trouble seeing as a possible suspect yet another person who had known Susan. Or perhaps there was some failing in me, and I was too easily taken in by men.

"Where do you live?"

"Oh, anyone can tell you. Ask Rick—or Carol. They can give you directions."

"All right, I'll come see you—tomorrow."

"Fantastic! And, Kathryn, don't let anyone tell you your sister did herself in. Not a chance, love, not a chance."

He was gone then, and I was alone, but Tony Greco soon found me, turning an amused look at Mike Campbell's departing back.

"So the local Don Juan has lost no time in finding you," he joked.

"He intimated that he was well-known, but not for what."

He laughed. "No, that reputation's only local. He is well-known, though, in art circles. He's a sculptor, and a very good one."

"Tony, I've got to talk to you. I found something, and I think it's important. And it's real this time, honest."

"Then you'll have to have dinner with me, because right now isn't a good time. People will be going over to the house after the funeral, and my presence there wouldn't look right."

"I thought you and Rick were friends."

"Oh, we went to school together, but socially we haven't mixed for years. It's just that my friends these days tend to be other bachelors. You know how it is."

"All right, dinner will be fine. What time?"

"About eight? Is that too late?"

"No, that's perfect. And, Tony, one other thing. My room was searched yesterday."

"Jesus, Katie, why didn't you call the police?"

"I don't know. Rick seemed reluctant, and then I just cleaned it up."

He heaved a sigh. "You're not helping me any by doing stuff like that, you know."

"I'm sorry. If anything else happens, I promise I'll call you."

He took a card out of his pocket and wrote something on it. "Here. This has my home phone as well as a direct line to me at the station. Keep it with you, okay?"

I nodded, and then Paul came by and asked me if I was ready to leave.

"So what did you think of Mike?" he asked me during the drive back to the house.

"You know him?"

"Hell, everyone knows Mike. He's the local character."

"He wants me to go see him tomorrow."

"Are you going?"

"Sure. He said he had something to tell me about Susan. Is there any reason I shouldn't go?"

"No, he's a good guy, really, and an exceptionally good sculptor. It would be worth your going just to see some of his work. He has shows in New York all the time, and the Museum of Modern Art bought one of his pieces."

I was impressed that the local Don Juan had time for all that and told Paul so.

He laughed. "Oh, he's serious most of the time. For the most part I think it's the women who chase him. I saw you talking to Tony. Did you tell him about your room being searched?"

"Yes, and he gave me hell for not calling the police."

"Yes, Carol and I gave Rick hell about it, too. It had to be an amateur, and there probably would have been fingerprints. And incidentally, I apologize again for not taking you seriously before. I think we're all convinced now that your sister didn't kill herself."

"Well, you had your reasons for thinking otherwise, Paul."

"Yeah, but I should have known better. I'll never forgive myself for not paying more attention to her symptoms."

We drove the rest of the way in silence while I thought to myself rather ironically that I had met more attractive men in two short days there than I had met in the past two years in California. I would have to keep reminding myself that my visit wasn't a social one and that I would be returning to California very soon. This reminded me that I should call my roommate and let her know I wouldn't be coming back quite yet, otherwise she would worry.

As though reading my thoughts, Paul broke the silence. "How about coming to the country club with me this weekend if you're still here? I remember your saying you played tennis, and the food there is excellent."

I laughed. "I was just thinking to myself that my visit was becoming far too social. I'm going to dinner with Tony tonight. Tomorrow I'm invited to visit the local Don

Juan. Now your invitation. But, yes, thanks, I'd love to if I'm still here. I feel in need of some exercise."

"Well, you know, you're the new girl in town and all that."

"Or else I remind everyone of Susan."

"I think I detect a trace of an inferiority complex coming out in you. Did Susan have that effect on you?"

"It was more her effect on men," I admitted.

"Well, I can't speak for Mike, but I know for a fact that Tony didn't know your sister. As for me, I wouldn't have invited Susan to play tennis even if she hadn't been married to my best friend. Women that aggressive put me off. To change the subject a bit, and it's none of my business, but I can't help noticing the way you look at Rick. Are you attracted to him?"

"It's *that* obvious? I must admit I was attracted to him the first time I met him. I think I saw him as the embodiment of all my romantic heroes. But that was a long time ago."

"I didn't know you had met before—he never mentioned it."

"It seems I made no impression on him," I said a bit ruefully.

"That's hard to believe."

"I was young then, and quite adoring—you know. As a doctor you must get your share of fans."

He laughed. "I just wanted to say—about Rick—well, he was pretty hurt by your sister. The fact that you look exactly like her wouldn't help you. I don't think anything could ever come of it."

"I know."

I must have sounded a bit sad, because he reached over

and patted me on the shoulder. "Don't despair, sweet Kathryn. You can have your pick from the rest of us."

We reached the house then and after that I was kept busy helping Carol and Mrs. Gurney serve coffee, tea, and food to the many guests who kept dropping by. At seven-thirty I excused myself to go upstairs and get ready for my date.

I quickly showered, then changed into the green dress and white sandals. Before going back downstairs, I went into Sara's room to say good night to her. She was in bed early, having missed her nap as a result of staying with neighbors while the funeral was being held.

She smiled at me in delight when I entered, holding out her arms to hug me. I was afraid she would want another story and I would have to disappoint her, something I didn't want to do, but she was very tired and quite content with just a hug and a kiss.

When I returned downstairs, Tony was having a drink with Rick and his parents, and I could see that Rick thought it was not quite right that I had changed my clothes and was preparing to go out. I ignored him while Tony finished his drink, then said my good-byes to Mr. and Mrs. Allison before leaving with Tony.

Chapter Nine

We drove along the coastal route. It was a lovely evening, and Tony had the top down on his Volkswagen convertible. I watched the waves coming in and, farther out, sailboats with their sails billowing in the breeze. His radio was tuned to a classical music station, and we drove for the most part without speaking. Our conversation was casual, mostly having to do with the scenery, with no mention of police business at all.

Tony was wearing a cream-colored summer suit, a dark-brown shirt, and a striped tie, and I was glad I had worn a dress. At home my date would have been dressed far more casually, probably in jeans, but I thought there was something to be said for not being casual all the time.

He pulled into the parking lot of a modern glass and wood restaurant called the Sandpiper, and an attendant parked the car.

The hostess led us out to a deck overlooking the water, where secluded tables were partially sheltered by large potted palms. In California, where the evenings are cool, I would have needed at least a sweater to sit outdoors, but here the variation in temperature between night and day was negligible.

I ordered a grasshopper, and the foamy green liquid

matched my dress, a fact that Tony noted at once. There was a candle on the table and a single white rose in a bud vase. Altogether it was a romantic setting complete with soft music in the background.

We ordered lobster, baked potatoes, and fresh spinach salads, and because Tony was not talking business, I decided to enjoy the dinner and wait until after coffee to bring up the subject of the ledger book.

He asked me what kind of work I did, and I told him about teaching high school English.

"You don't look like any English teacher *I* ever had," he teased me.

"That's because you didn't go to school in California."

"Do all the teachers out there look like you?"

"Yes. Everyone in California is a blond."

He laughed. "I might try to get on the force out there."

"I think you'd like it. I know you'd like the weather—in addition to all the blonds."

"I like you—that's enough."

We were having an after-dinner liqueur by then, and I thought that if I didn't bring up the subject of police business soon, I might never get the chance. Tony was beginning to act very romantic, and the way I was feeling after two grasshoppers, a bottle of wine with dinner, and an after-dinner liqueur made me think that if I didn't put a stop to it soon, I probably never would.

I reached into my handbag and pulled out the ledger book, handing it to him across the table.

He opened it, then took out his reading glasses to get a better look. He shrugged and raised a quizzical brow at me.

"It's a ledger book," I told him.

"No kidding!"

"My sister kept it hidden between the mattress and box spring of Sara's bed. Sara gets me confused with her mother and got it out for me last night."

He looked at the book again. "Well, I recognize some of the names, but do you know what it's for?"

"I thought *you* could tell me that. Incidentally, it's not in her writing."

"That makes it more interesting." He called the waiter over and ordered a pot of coffee for us.

"I think there's something you should know. My sister was selling drugs."

"You're full of information tonight. I bet you were busting to tell me that all through dinner."

"Not at all. I wouldn't have spoiled that beautiful dinner for anything."

He chuckled, and his eyes were warm as they looked at me. He really was a very sexy man, and his appeal was further enhanced by the fact that, as police chief, he was probably the only man around that I could trust.

"How did you find out about her selling drugs?"

"I can't tell you that."

"You can't or you won't?"

"I refuse to reveal my source."

He laughed. "That's only for investigative reporters. With you it's withholding information, and I could drag you into court."

I smiled at him, enjoying the banter. "Drag me into court, Tony."

"I don't need to, Katie. You got that little piece of information from none other than Johnny Fowler."

"What makes you think so?"

"Don't worry, I'm not going to hassle the kid over a few

pills. It just stands to reason he was the one who told you—you don't know that many people here."

"The names in the book—who are they?"

He frowned. "That's the problem. Most of them are respectable businessmen in town. But then the book could be perfectly innocent."

"Then why would she have hidden it?"

"That's the problem. Now maybe this book is drug-related and maybe it isn't. It could be your sister was having affairs with these men and then blackmailing them. Not one on the list is unmarried."

I gave him a doubtful look. "That many affairs? How would she find the time?"

"Well, they didn't have to be simultaneous."

I considered that and decided it was possible. "It's too bad, Tony, that news has gotten around about Susan's death. Otherwise you could send me around to see those men and find out something."

"Yeah, well, the news is out, and one of those guys could be a killer. I don't want you risking your life, Katie."

"So what are you going to do?"

"Have my men talk to the guys on the list; lean on them a little. One of them will talk—they always do."

"I imagine that book was the reason my room was searched. After all, Rick and Paul were the only ones there when I said I found a journal."

"The way I see it, Katie, if it was blackmail, then whoever searched your room could have been any one of these guys. But if it's something else, like drugs, then the person who searched your room was the person who kept this book. And that might be more difficult."

"Listen, Tony, it couldn't have been blackmail, or it would be in Susan's handwriting."

He ran his fingers through his hair. "Sorry, I'm just not thinking clearly. Let's go someplace where we can dance."

"That's it? The police business is over?"

"We could stay here and talk it to death, but I don't think we'll get anywhere until my men do some investigating. Or we can go to a lovely little spot I know about and dance the night away. What'll it be, Katie?"

I stood up. "By all means, let's dance."

His idea of a "lovely little spot" was the most raucous discotheque I had ever been in. It was just as well, considering it lessened the romantic atmosphere he had created, and anyway, I like to dance.

The disco was little, raunchy, and very, very warm. There was a young crowd, mostly teen-agers, and a few older ones who looked college age.

The dance floor was the usual minute square, and the tables looked like tree trunks, and probably were. I never got close enough to one to find out, as they were all taken. The stereo system, though, was excellent, and I decided that if Tony could stand it, so could I.

The bar was less crowded than the tables, and Tony seated me on one of the stools before excusing himself to go to the men's room.

The bartender, a benign-looking guy of about forty, came over. I was about to order a beer, preferring something less alcoholic, when he leaned over to me in a very familiar manner and said, "What are you doing with the police chief?"

It didn't take a genius to figure out he had known Susan and hadn't yet heard of her death. I wondered who she had come there with; the place wasn't really her style. I decided that any information I could find out about her activities might help Tony in his investigation, so I played along.

I winked at him in the way I had seen Susan do on many occasions. "Don't get uptight—he's a family friend."

He gave me a look of sly admiration. "Jesus, that's a good cover! Hey, did you pass along my complaint?"

"Sure did."

"And?"

I began to think I was really onto something and hoped Tony wouldn't return too quickly. "Sorry," I told him, "I haven't gotten an answer yet."

His unhappy expression at my news suddenly changed to a big smile, and he asked me what I'd like to drink. Then Tony returned. We both ordered a beer, and I was anxious to tell him what had happened, but the bartender stayed close by, so I didn't risk it.

"This crowd makes me feel ancient," I remarked to Tony.

"You? You don't look any older than the others here. I'm the old man in the crowd."

"How old are you?"

"Thirty-five my next birthday."

"Well, come on, old man. Let me see if you can still dance."

I could see he wasn't eager, but I wanted to tell him about the bartender. I took his hand and literally pulled him off the barstool. We found an unoccupied few inches on the dance floor, but I found the music was too loud to do any talking.

Tony wasn't much of a disco dancer. He moved better walking than he did dancing, but there wasn't enough room to do much, anyway. I saw Johnny Fowler across the floor with a pretty auburn-haired girl, and waved to him. I thought he saw me but wasn't positive, because right after I waved, a couple blocked my view of him.

The sandals I was wearing weren't good for dancing. They were backless, and my heels kept slipping over. It was also very warm. I was glad when the song changed to a slow tune and I could relax a little.

Tony pulled me close to him, and I found that while the music was still just as loud, my mouth was now only inches away from his ear, and he was able to hear me.

"Who's the bartender?" I asked him.

He gave me an affronted look. "What is this? I leave you alone for two minutes and now you're interested in Shel Corbett."

"Is that his name?"

"Yeah, but he's not exactly a bartender—he owns the place."

"Well, he thought I was Susan."

"Your sister got around."

"Stop joking—I'm serious. I think she was his supplier or whatever you call it."

"What did he say?"

I repeated my conversation to him, and he broke out in a grin and kissed me on the nose. "My scheme worked," he said jubilantly.

"What scheme? What are you talking about? I was the one who was smart enough to play along with him and pretend I was Susan."

"But I set it up."

I stopped dancing and gave him an indignant look. "You set me up?"

"Keep dancing—you look funny just standing there."

92

I moved back into his arms. "All right, but start explaining."

"His name was in the ledger book, and I thought there just might be a chance, since this place is a couple of towns over from Cauley, that he hadn't heard of your sister's death."

"Are you going to take him in for questioning?"

"On what evidence?"

"Well, his name is in the book."

"That's no crime—we don't even know what the book's for."

"Well . . . it's suspicious, isn't it?"

"Katie, according to the Supreme Court, citizens have rights. Didn't you know that?"

I must have looked crestfallen, because he patted me on the back and said, "Cheer up, I'll have one of my men pay him a visit in the morning. But I doubt he knows anything."

"Why not?"

"Because it looks as though your sister was the middleman."

"Middlewoman," I corrected him with a disdainful look.

He laughed. "Will you settle for middleperson? Anyway, I'd lay odds that no one on that list knew who she was dealing for."

"But if she was the only one who knew, and she's—she's dead,—then we'll never find out."

I must have sounded a little tearful, because he stopped talking and just held me close for a while. It was comforting, and I felt in need of it. Part of me felt it wasn't right to be out dancing on the night of Susan's funeral, but if it would help to find out what had really happened to her, it would be worth it. That was the important thing.

"It sure is a perfect setup," I said to Tony as the music changed over to another slow dance.

"You mean the disco?"

"Yes. If he's selling to kids, it's a perfect place."

He nodded. "That's what struck me about the list. They were all businessmen, but all their businesses brought them into contact with kids."

"What kind of businesses?"

"There's a drive-in hamburger place that's popular with the kids, a bowling alley, a sporting goods store—just to name a few."

"That's terrible."

"Yes, it is."

"That would be like me selling drugs because I come in contact with a lot of kids teaching high school."

"Don't think *that* isn't done, too."

I glanced over at the bar to get another look at the kind of man who made money off selling drugs to kids, and I froze. The bartender was talking to Johnny, and they were looking over at me. Then, as I watched, the bartender turned livid and slammed his fist down on the bar. A crowd of kids started to gather in front of him, and I saw Johnny get his girl and head for the door.

"Let's get out of here, Tony." Apparently the bartender hadn't appreciated hearing about my impersonation, and I was afraid there would be trouble.

Tony turned to see what I was staring at. "What happened?"

"He was talking to Johnny Fowler, and I think Johnny told him who I really am."

"Damn! I don't want any trouble with those kids. Come on."

As we passed the bar to go out the door, several boys turned to stare at us. Tony hustled me out so fast, I almost lost a shoe, but when I protested, he wouldn't let up.

"Fasten your seat belt," he ordered me as he started the engine.

He pulled out of the parking lot in a hurry, but even so, several boys came running out of the disco and piled into a large Buick. As we turned onto the highway the Buick wasn't far behind us. The coastal road back to Cauley was narrow, with cliffs on one side that dropped off sharply to rocks below, and fog was rolling in. It wasn't enough to really obscure our vision, but occasionally we hit a thick pocket of it and had to slow down.

I turned around in my seat as far as the seat belt would allow and watched the car behind us. "It's gaining on us, Tony." I was beginning to be frightened.

"They're only kids—they're just trying to scare us."

"I don't know. It would be pretty stupid of them to try to scare the police chief. What if they try to run us off the road?" It didn't seem to me that a small VW, particularly a convertible, could stand a chance against a heavy Buick.

"They won't run me off the road." I tried to feel as confident as he sounded, but it didn't work.

The Buick was so close to us by then that I could see the driver. It started to pull over beside us, and I was really starting to panic when I heard a low chuckle from Tony.

"Watch this, Katie."

He floored the accelerator, and it was like taking off in a jet. We shot forward and within seconds put enough distance between us and the Buick to allow me to sink back in my seat with relief.

"A Volkswagen did that?"

"Would you believe a Porsche engine?"

I managed a small laugh. "I was really scared back there. I had visions of us going over the cliff."

He reached over and took my hand. "You're trembling."

"What are you going to do about them?" I turned around in the seat, but even though he had slowed down considerably, I didn't see a car anywhere behind us.

"I don't plan on doing anything to them. They're good kids, basically. We have very little juvenile delinquency around here. What I want to do is something for them. Like locking up the bastards who sell them drugs."

What he said didn't need a comment. I thought how lucky the town was to have such a good man working for it.

He turned to me with a smile. "Enough of that serious talk. Now, would you like to go to a quieter place where we can dance without incident?"

I squeezed his hand. "Thanks, but no. I think I'd like to go home. I don't really feel right about being out on the night of my sister's funeral, but I had to talk to you and give you the ledger book, and I didn't want the others around when I did it."

"Gee, and I thought it was my charm and good looks."

"I really don't think you need assurance on either of those points."

He turned serious. "Tell me, Katie, were you and your sister close?"

I didn't know how to answer that. As children we had been—but that was more a matter of proximity than being compatible. Then, for a period after our parents' deaths, we had drawn closer together. But it had been several years since I had seen her, and I didn't think I could truthfully describe us as being close.

"Not really. I think we were too dissimilar to be close. Also, Susan always hated being a twin."

"Did you hate it, too?"

"Not really. I think if we had really been alike—in temperament—I would have loved it. But I'm not saying she was wrong and I was right. I think she had a much better image of herself and was a stronger person."

"Don't downgrade yourself, Katie."

"I'm glad you never knew her." It came out sounding more vehement than I had meant.

"Why is that?"

"Oh, Tony, it's really been difficult being here. I want to mourn my sister, but then I see how she treated her child and was involved with drugs, and no one seemed to like her. And they all look at me and see *her*, and I'll never be anything to them but just an extension of her . . . ."

I started crying then, and he stopped the car and turned off the engine.

"Don't stop—it's not safe," I said, but then I looked out the window and saw that we were home.

Tony put his arms around me and placed my head on his shoulder. It wasn't comfortable, as the gear shift was in the way, but I couldn't seem to stop crying.

"It's okay, Katie, let it all out."

"No—nobody—cries for her, Tony," I sobbed. "Maybe Sara would, but—but she doesn't even know about her mother. Nobody cares."

Finally I wore myself down and was able to lift my head and speak more coherently. "I'm sorry about that, Tony."

"Don't be. You don't have to apologize for caring."

"Mostly I've been holding it all in. If they had grieved, I would have joined them, but—"

"How did Rick feel about your sister?"

"I think he hated her. And he certainly doesn't like me, because I remind him of her."

"Do you think he hated her enough to kill her?"

"I don't know. At first, when he was trying to convince me she killed herself, I thought it was possible. What do you think? You know him better than I do."

"If I've learned anything in this business, it's that the most unlikely people are capable of murder. Perhaps we all are. I know one thing, though. In a case like this, the husband is the logical suspect. And if he had a good reason—"

"Like jealousy?"

"Yeah, like jealousy." He shifted in the seat. "Look, hon, I want to spell it all out for you, so you'll be careful. If Rick did it, you're probably not in any danger. He might try to scare you into going back home, but it isn't likely he'll kill again. If he did kill her, it was probably in the heat of anger. Husbands rarely cold-bloodedly plot to kill their wives. But if he didn't kill her, it's a whole other ball game. As for the drugs, when it's just pills and maybe some marijuana, there usually aren't killings involved. We're not dealing with organized crime and the hard stuff—at least I doubt it. But if it was a fairly big operation —and judging by the amounts shown in that ledger book, it was lucrative—and your sister was posing some kind of threat to someone, well, in that case, you could be in danger, particularly if the party thinks you know something."

"What do I do?"

"I don't suppose you'd consider going home."

"No."

"Did you tell anyone about the ledger book?"

"Just you."

"Good. Keep it that way. Just act dumb, like you don't know anything. And please, don't trust anybody."

"What about my talking to that bartender tonight?"

"He didn't really say anything incriminating. And he obviously only had contact with your sister. Anyway, he wouldn't be so stupid as to let the news get out that he was taken in by you."

It was good talking to Tony—actually just being with him. He made me feel safe. "I think I'd better go in now. Thanks, Tony—for the dinner and everything else."

"My pleasure. And, Katie, I'll keep in close touch. If anything strange happens—"

"I'll call you, don't worry."

His arms were still around me, but he released me then, and I got out of the car. "You don't need to walk me up to the house." I leaned through the window and gave him a quick kiss. "Good night, Tony."

"Good night, Katie." He let out a low chuckle. "And don't think you'll get away with a sisterly kiss next time."

He waited until I was inside the screened porch before driving away. I had my hand on the doorknob to let myself in when Rick's voice spoke out of the darkness.

"Did you have a good time?" I looked around and could vaguely make out his shape on the glider.

"Yes, thank you. We had a nice dinner."

He gave a nasty laugh. "Tony hasn't changed much since high school, I see. He still makes out with girls in his car."

I was furious at his insinuation. "How dare you say such a thing to me. Tony's more of a gentleman than you'll ever be! How many innocent young girls has *he* gotten pregnant, Rick?" I heard a gasp from him, but didn't wait around for a reply. I opened the door, slammed it behind me, and ran up the stairs to my room.

I had bad dreams again that night. But instead of being pushed off a cliff, I dreamt I was with Tony in his car, and the Buick forced us over the side of the cliff.

Chapter Ten

Early the next morning I opened my eyes, tried to sit up, and sank back with a groan. I felt as though the sunlight had seared my tired eyes, and my head felt twice its usual size. I could tell I was not going to be my usual cheerful self that morning, and I also knew that the one thing that might straighten me out would be a good run on the beach. Before that good run, however, I wanted to just rest for a little while . . . .

The next time I awakened, my condition hadn't improved, but I got up anyway. Splashing cold water on my face and brushing my teeth helped a little, but not much.

I looked for my jeans and T-shirt, but couldn't find them anywhere. I remembered tossing them on the floor in the closet, meaning to get them washed later on. I was embarrassed to think that maybe Mrs. Gurney had taken them for laundering—I didn't want to be an extra burden on her or have her think I expected to be waited on.

I tried to think of what else I could jog in, and the only thing I could come up with was a bikini with my pajama top for a jacket.

I got into my bathing suit and running shoes, then put my pajama top back on. It was of a light-blue chambray, and with the sleeves rolled up, it could conceivably be taken for beachwear.

I went down the stairs quietly, not wanting to see anyone until my mood had improved, and let myself out the back door. Mrs. Gurney wasn't in the kitchen, but the door leading down to the basement was open, and I supposed she was down there. I desperately needed a cup of coffee but thought it best to run on an empty stomach.

Going down the stone steps to the beach, I could feel each of them jolt right up to my head. You are clearly not a drinker, I told myself, so in the future be a little more moderate.

The smell of the ocean always does something for me. That morning, the closer I got to it, the more I seemed to recover.

At the bottom of the steps I did a few kneebends to warm up, then reached my arms to the sky and thanked God for making oceans and beaches. With nothing more on my mind than a quick two-mile run, I turned—and let out a scream that almost drowned out the sound of the waves.

There, on the beach, where my sister had been found, was a body. It was sprawled facedown in the sand, and I saw jeans and blond hair. I couldn't tell whether it was male or female, but from the position of the body, I was sure whoever it was hadn't survived. I don't know how long I stood there, my senses stunned, before I turned back to the steps and ran all the way up, crying for help with every breath.

Eventually my voice must have carried to the top of the cliffs, because by the time I reached the top stair and collapsed on the grass, Rick and Carol and Mrs. Gurney were beside me.

I was fighting to get my breath. They kept asking me what was the matter, but all I could do was shake my head and point back down the stairs.

Rick finally got the message and started down, and Carol sat on the ground beside me.

"What happened, Katie? Did something happen to you on the beach?"

I tried to speak. My voice was hoarse and my throat sore, but I managed to tell her that there was a body on the beach.

She and Mrs. Gurney exchanged stricken looks, and Carol got up. She was about to go down when Rick appeared at the top of the stairs.

"I want all of you to come down and see this," he said wearily.

"Oh, Rick, no," pleaded his sister, but he held up a hand to quiet her.

"It's not a dead body, Carol, just a cruel joke. But I'm sure we're all going to be questioned about it, and I think we all should see it."

We went down, and I stood with the others, looking down at the sand-stuffed clothes and the wig placed over a rock, and the horror I had been feeling was slowly replaced with anger.

"It was just a joke—a prank played by some kid," was Rick's opinion.

"Then the kid has a sick sense of humor," I muttered, and saw Carol and Mrs. Gurney nod in agreement.

Rick started to reach down and pick up the wig.

"Don't!" I said loudly. "Don't touch it. I want Tony to see this."

He looked at the others as though to say, "Let's humor her," but I ignored him. I was staring at the jeans. There was something familiar about them—yes—the way they had been cut off at the bottom and then overstitched instead of hemmed.

I looked at the housekeeper. "Mrs. Gurney, did you by any chance take any dirty clothes out of my closet to be washed?"

She gave me a look of surprise. "Why, no, miss. I wouldn't go in your closet without asking. But if you need some clothes washed—"

"What about you, Carol?"

"Of course not, Katie. Why do you ask?"

"Because my jeans and T-shirt were missing this morning, and I believe those are mine." I pointed to the clothes on the effigy.

And then some of the terror came back mixed with anger. I turned, outraged, to Rick.

"Why is this happening to me in your house? First my room is searched, and you don't do anything about it. Now this happens, and you treat it as a joke. I feel like I've been violated. Someone seems to have access to my room, to my things—even to me—and you do nothing!"

A pulse in his temple was throbbing as he stared down at me coldly, his eyes hard and brilliant. "Are you accusing me, Kathryn?"

I took a deep breath before I spoke and willed myself to remain calm. "I find it hard to believe that some outsider would have such easy entry to your house or know which room I'm staying in or even which clothes are mine. It looks to me like a warning, Rick. A message clearly stated: 'Get out—go back to California.' "

Mrs. Gurney was distressed, and Carol was looking uneasily from me to Rick and back to me again.

"I wonder that you would remain in the house of such

104

a monster," Rick said coldly. "First I killed my wife, and now I'm threatening you. Is that correct? I like this as little as you do, Kathryn. I value my privacy. And, of course, *I* know I'm innocent. If you'll excuse me, I'll phone the police."

Mrs. Gurney put her arm around me. "Come along, dear. You haven't had any breakfast—not even a cup of coffee."

I sat down shakily on the sand. "No, you go on up—I'll be up in a few minutes. I still want to do some running."

"You all right, Katie?" Carol asked me anxiously.

"I'm okay. Go on. I'll be right up, really."

Mrs. Gurney started back up the steps, but Carol joined me on the sand.

"I'll watch you while you run. I should join you, but I'm not feeling that ambitious."

I looked at her wrist to see if she was wearing a watch. "Good, you can time me, okay? Let me know when I've been running fifteen minutes."

"Right."

It was a monotonous run, up and down the small stretch of beach, and the constant turning really slowed me down. But after a few minutes, I felt a lot better and knew I was sweating the hangover out of my system. After about ten minutes, I made the turn and saw that Tony was talking to Carol and that two other men were kneeling down beside the effigy. Tony looked up and waved to me, and I ran over and joined them.

"It hasn't been a great morning," I complained to him. "First I wake up with a hangover, and then this."

He didn't smile at my attempt at humor. "You're sure those are your clothes, Katie?"

"The jeans are, and I'm assuming the T-shirt is also. They were both missing from my closet this morning."

"It must have been done last night—the clothes are still damp. I'm afraid we're going to have to take them to the lab, but they'll be returned later."

"That's okay. Actually I could live without seeing them again."

I decided to go back up to the house and put some clothes on. Carol and I were starting up the steps when Tony yelled to me, "Don't go away—we'll be up soon to ask a few questions. And, Katie—I like your pajama top."

"I thought it was a beach shirt," said Carol.

"That's what you were supposed to think." I laughed.

I took a quick shower, washed my hair, and blew it dry. I dressed in a pair of purple cotton pants and a fuchsia T-shirt. I was tan enough by then that I could get away with vivid colors, and I really loved them.

Tony's men weren't around when I got back downstairs, but Tony was eating breakfast with the others, and I smiled at Mrs. Gurney gratefully when she put a plate piled high with bacon and eggs in front of me and a steaming mug of coffee.

"I just don't know how to explain it, Tony," Rick was saying when I came down. "Carol and I were here last night, and my parents and Paul—and Sara, of course. They stayed on after the funeral, and we all had a late supper. The folks left about ten, and Paul left shortly before you brought Kathryn home. He and I were talking out on the front porch—Carol had gone in to watch the eleven o'clock news. We rarely lock up the house, and there are several doors in, but I can't see someone taking that chance. I know all this makes me look very suspicious, but I can't help it."

106

"There were a lot of people here earlier," Carol remarked.

Tony turned to me. "When did you first realize your clothes were missing?"

"Not until this morning. But they could have been missing yesterday, and I wouldn't have noticed."

Rick shook his head. "I'm sorry, but I just can't see any of those people doing it. They were all old friends."

Tony's tone became more businesslike. "Yes, but someone did it, Rick."

I looked around at them. "Well, if you want to be logical, I could have done it the easiest. How come you didn't think of that, Rick?"

He looked amused. "Oh, I thought of it."

Carol gave us both a look of mock disgust. Or maybe I just thought it was mock and she was really serious. "What about Johnny Fowler, Tony? He and his parents were here after the funeral, and he's seen Katie down at the beach."

"He would have no reason to do it," I said positively. "And it had to be someone who knew I was using that room. After all, it used to be your room, Carol. I think most people would assume I would be in a guest room."

"That does make us look very suspicious." Carol sighed.

"Oh, Carol—no one would suspect you for a moment," I said tactlessly. I glanced at Rick to see if I should apologize, but he looked amused.

Tony leaned back in his chair and lighted a cigarette. "Well, we'll take the clothes down to the lab and see if they'll tell us anything. Incidentally, what about the wig? Any idea where that came from?"

"I forgot all about the wig," I said. "I don't own one. Did Susan?"

Rick shook his head. "Not that I know of—I've never seen one around."

"I never saw her wearing one," volunteered Carol.

"Someone could have taken the clothes and then come back later with the wig," said Tony.

"That's ridiculous," I muttered.

He grinned at me. "Then you come up with a better idea."

Rick got up and excused himself, saying he had to get to work, but Tony stopped him before he left. "Rick, I know it's usually not necessary to lock houses around here at night, but I'd appreciate it if you'd lock up, at least for the remainder of Katie's stay."

"I would have anyway, Tony," Rick told him, then headed out of the room to his study.

"It doesn't look good for him, does it, Tony?" Carol asked.

"No, and he doesn't help by being so uncooperative."

Carol sighed. "I swear, if I didn't know him so well, I'd think he was doing all these things. It seems to point to him."

Tony looked uncertain. "Well . . ."

"I know what you're going to say, Tony," Carol cut in. "I'm sure the families of murderers all feel the same way. But you grew up with him. Can you believe him capable of it?"

"I'll tell you, Carol, I can't believe any brother of yours would be capable of it."

"That didn't answer my question."

"Well, it will have to do."

I didn't like Carol being put in the position where she

had to defend her brother, so I changed the subject. "I'm going over to see Mike Campbell this afternoon. Can either of you tell me how to get there?"

"Who's Mike Campbell?" asked Carol.

Tony laughed. "You must be the only female within miles who doesn't know the answer to that. But I guess he arrived since you've been living in Boston. Anyway, he's a sculptor, and quite a well-known one at that."

"What does he look like?" she asked.

"Oh, he's a big bear of a man," I answered her. "Lots of red hair and a beard."

"Were you talking to him at the cemetery?"

"Yes."

"I saw him. I meant to ask you about him, and then I forgot all about it. Did he know Susan?"

"So it seems. But what was really surprising was that he knew who I was. She had talked to him about me."

"Hmmmm, he sounds very interesting. I'd go along with you, but I promised I'd take Sara down to the beach this afternoon," said Carol.

Tony had taken a pen and a note pad out of his pocket and now handed me what he had been writing. "Here, Katie. These are directions to his place. It's not far, and I don't think you'll have any trouble finding it. Are you taking Rick's car?"

I shook my head. "No, I rented one at the airport in Boston."

"You really should return that," Carol told me. "It's going to cost you a fortune, and you don't really need one here. You can always use mine or Rick's."

"Yes, but I'll need a way back to the airport when I leave."

"Sorry to interrupt, ladies, but I must get back to

work." Tony stood up, and I walked him to the door. "Take care now," he cautioned me before he left, and I promised that I would.

Carol was still at the breakfast table, and we had another cup of coffee together.

"I've been thinking, Katie. Why don't we drive into Boston Friday and return your car? I have a friend there I'd like to invite down for the weekend, and he can drive us back. As for getting to the airport when you leave, I'll be glad to drive you in. I'd also like you to see my apartment."

"I haven't heard about this friend before," I teased her. "Tell me about him."

She blushed. "His name's Quentin Harding, and he teaches at Harvard—anthropology. Anyway, I've been seeing him for a while, and I'd like Rick to meet him."

"Anything serious?"

"I don't know, Katie. It's not the great romance of the century, if that's what you mean."

"Was it love at first sight?"

"No, I didn't even like him when I first met him. But he grows on you."

I shook my head and made a face at her. "Doesn't sound exciting to me. I fear you're no romantic, Carol."

She looked surprised. "I wouldn't have taken you for one. You seem very practical to me."

"Anyone teaching English Literature is a romantic," I insisted.

"Anyway, what do you think?" You really ought to see Boston while you're here, and it would do you good to get out for a day."

"I'd love to. And I'm dying to see your romantic hero."

"All right, Katie, that's enough of that nonsense," she said, blushing again.

Later I went with her to pick up Sara at her nursery school. The school was in a private home and run by two young mothers who had wanted to find playmates for their only children. When we arrived, Sara was playing house in a large packing crate with a tow-headed little boy and was clearly not thrilled to see us. Nevertheless, we induced her with promises of the beach, and she finally got out and came home with us. Whatever my sister's reasons for putting Sara in a nursery school, I thought it was a good idea and beneficial for her to be with other children instead of adults all the time.

We stopped off in town and picked up a few groceries for Mrs. Gurney, then went home and sat talking on the terrace until lunchtime, after which I went to see Mike Campbell.

Chapter Eleven

I followed Tony's directions to Mike Campbell's studio and, after driving several miles, was surprised to note that I was heading away from the ocean. I had pictured him living at the beach, but instead I was driving into a rural, woody area.

When I arrived at what should have been my destination, if I had followed the directions correctly, I was in front of a quaint steepled church surrounded on three sides by woods. I was about to go on when I noticed a wooden sign driven into the ground which read, CAMPBELL.

I got out and was halfway to the door when it opened and Mike came charging out, full of exuberance, and lifted me off my feet with a bear hug. He was wearing jeans and was shirtless, displaying a massive chest covered with curly red hair. From his head to his dirty bare feet, he was covered with white dust.

When he released me, I was covered with it, too, but I didn't care; it was terrific being made to feel so welcome.

"Somehow I didn't imagine you lived in a church," I told him.

"One thing a sculptor needs is space, Kathryn, and most New England houses are measly little things. This couldn't be more perfect if I had designed it myself. But welcome, luv. I'm glad to see you here. And I apologize for covering your clothes with my dust. Ah, you Californians, you dress so colorfully. New Englanders seem to feel it's a sin to dress in anything that isn't drab."

He took me inside, and when I looked around, trying to take it all in, my first thought was that it was a Disneyland for adults. Or perhaps I should amend that to say for adult art-lovers.

He had retained the church's stained-glass windows, which extended upward for almost three stories, and his sculptures were all done in white marble, so that the light as it played through the windows and touched upon the marble was like a kaleidoscope. The sculptures were full of motion, and with this added effect, they seemed to be alive.

He dealt in beauty, form, and a little bit of fantasy. The sculptures were all bigger than life-size, nobler and far more beautiful.

As I gazed in wonder he watched me, a pleased expression on his face. He laughed out loud when I went over to a giant unicorn and ran my hand along its back. It was incredibly soft to the touch, smooth and somewhat warm. It seemed alive, ready to dash off at any instant. I longed to climb on its back, but it was too high. As though reading my thoughts, Mike came over and gently eased me up on the creature's back. There was something about the feel of that marble that kept making me want to rub my hands over it, and I saw that as Mike walked around he couldn't help feeling the sculptures as he passed them.

From the vantage point of the unicorn's back, I looked around some more. There was a dragon curled around in a half circle in one corner of the room, and piled against the dragon's belly were giant-size stuffed pillows covered in multicolored fabrics. In another corner was a flat-topped toadstool with smaller toadstools grouped around it. I began to see that he had fashioned even his furniture out of marble; that he inhabited a fantasy world.

"I love it—I love them all," I told him quite truthfully, "but do the galleries really sell these? Who buys unicorns and dragons and fairies and such?"

"No, these are just for myself. For the galleries, I do more serious work—more abstract. But I'll tell you a secret—I'm really more serious about these. Don't tell anyone; it would ruin my reputation."

I laughed in delight at his admission. Then I noticed the bed and wondered why I hadn't seen it before. It was really just a mattress on top of a wooden platform, but the whole thing was suspended from the high ceiling by chains so that it could swing back and forth. On the bed, on top of what looked like a handmade patchwork quilt, was a sculpture of a nude woman—a very familiar-looking nude woman. I knew at once that it was Susan, and so, of course, it could also be me. I felt myself flush.

He was watching my reaction and laughed. "You're thinking it could be you, aren't you? Well, don't be embarrassed—how could such beauty embarrass you?"

It *was* beautiful, one of the most beautiful works of art I had ever seen, and I couldn't tear my eyes away from it. It looked so soft, so inviting that I wanted to go over to it and rub my hands along its length, but that thought was so narcissistic that I thrust it from my mind. I thought of Susan posing for it, then scolded myself for being such a prude. He was an artist, after all, and used to seeing women in the nude.

"How about a cup of coffee?" he asked me.

"In a place like this you should serve nectar at the very least," I admonished him.

"Ummm, and it's only instant at that."

"I'll take a cup—gladly."

I managed to slide off the back of the unicorn by myself and joined him in the kitchen—another surprise. It was a room made for serious cooking, with dozens of copper pans hanging over the stove, shelves of cookbooks, and the latest appliances, including a microwave oven. Caught in the act of grinding coffee beans, he grinned at me.

"You're spoiling me," I told him. "Instant would have been fine."

"Maybe for you—it's myself I'm spoiling. I can't stand instant coffee or fast foods."

We drank our coffee out on his patio. It was very quiet, and I kept straining to hear the ocean, but we were too far away. A gray-and-white cat appeared and rubbed against my legs, then jumped into Mike's lap.

"What did you want to talk to me about?" I finally asked him, beginning to wonder why he had invited me to visit.

"Rumor has it that Susan killed herself, and I just wanted to disabuse you of that notion."

"I never believed that for a moment. She wasn't the type."

"No, not her. She was too full of life. She was a bit homesick, though."

"Homesick? But we hadn't had a home for years—and her home was here."

"I mean for California. She talked on and on about it; she really didn't care for New England. She was always telling me she had an urge to get into a car and just race down one of the freeways. Didn't like the roads here—said she could never get up enough speed."

"Well, she would have been disappointed. The speed limit has been fifty-five out there ever since the last gasoline crisis."

"And she hated all the rain. She said in California it only rained one time of the year, and then not very much. When she got tired of the rain, she said she would drive to Palm Springs and get away from it. Tell me, is it true? Does it never rain in sunny California?"

I laughed. "Well, hardly ever. Certainly not in the summer. I'll tell you what *I* don't like about New England, and that's the humidity."

"None of us is crazy about that. Most of all, your sister hated the winters. She kept asking when the sun was coming out again."

"I think it might be hard to uproot Californians—we are used to perfection."

"She didn't like the people here, either—at least for the most part. She said they were too conservative and stuffy, not friendly and open like those back home."

I didn't say anything to that. For the most part, I had found the people very friendly, and I surmised that the women here hadn't been friendly with my sister. But she had never been open and friendly with women herself, at least not when I had known her. She had never had female friends and had done her best to antagonize mine.

Mike leaned over to set his cup down on the ground, and the cat made a swipe at his moving beard. "Little rascal—thinks he's the boss and I'm only here to serve him. She talked a lot about you, too, Kathryn."

"It surprised me when you knew who I was. You seem

116

to be the only one here who ever heard of me. Rick knew that she had a sister, but he didn't know we were twins."

"Oh, I know all about you. She used to regale me with stories about your childhood and about switching places with you."

He related a few incidents, times when Susan had pretended to be me. I had not known at the time, however, and now some strange incidents I remembered from my youth suddenly made sense to me. Perhaps her escapades could be considered amusing in retrospect, but at the time I hadn't thought so.

"What about her marriage, Mike? Did she talk at all about that? I just can't understand why she couldn't make a go of it."

"I think that partly her expectations of being a famous writer's wife weren't realistic. She envisioned publishers' parties in New York, being interviewed for magazines, meeting lots of famous people—you know the route. Rather like being married to a movie star. But the truth of the matter is, a writer leads a solitary life, especially if he's a serious writer, which Mr. Allison appears to be. Have you read any of his books?"

I nodded. "All of them. I think he's the best American writer today."

"Yes, I think he just might be—he's right up there with a handful of others, anyway. You know she did take most of the blame for the bad marriage. She admitted that in a sense she had tricked him into it. Not that the baby wasn't his, she didn't mean that. And she did love her child—can't blame her. That Sara is a little charmer."

"You've met Sara?"

"Susan and I thought I should get acquainted with her—since I was going to be her new daddy."

He let it drop casually, but I was stunned. I hadn't even contemplated something like that. "You—you and Susan were going to get married?"

"Well, now, I didn't say married, did I? I'm leaving for Italy in September—going to stay there a year. Susan wanted to come along and bring the child. She really did love her, but on the other hand she wasn't too big on mothering. But she wouldn't leave her behind—didn't want Rick to have her. I was willing. I like little ones."

I thought about that for a minute. If Rick knew that she was leaving him, and not only taking Sara but taking her far enough away so that he wouldn't be able to see her, well, that would be a pretty strong motive, particularly if she taunted him with it.

"Why are you going to Italy?"

"Would you believe I've never been to Europe? And why would an artist want to go to Italy? Can you think of a better place? I want to see every painting and every sculpture and every church—just soak it all up. I've been working solitarily long enough. Now I want to see what the rest of the world is doing."

"It sounds wonderful. I'd love to see Europe, too."

"So come along with me, Kathryn."

He sounded perfectly serious. I waited for him to laugh or make a joke of it, but he sat there contemplating me seriously.

"As a substitute for Susan?"

"Not at all. I find you two completely different. Come along—we'll have a grand time. I have friends there, and they're finding me a villa where I can work. Evenings we can sit in some sidewalk café and talk and drink and—just live! And, Kathryn," he added as an inducement, "I hear the weather there is just like that of California."

118

I laughed at that. "Don't think you're not tempting me, Mike. But, no—it's not possible. Aside from the fact that we're complete strangers, I've signed a teaching contract for the fall. I also have a roommate who depends on me for half the rent. And I guess I'm just not as adventurous as my sister."

"Well, don't say no now. At least think about it."

"Did you love my sister?"

"We weren't in love, if that's what you mean. I love my work, and it comes first with me—always will. I imagine her husband was the same way. But we were good friends and got on well together. I found her very bright and amusing, never boring. But I imagine it would only have lasted the one year in Italy. She couldn't take my quiet life here any more than she could with her husband. I think she would have returned to California eventually."

I didn't ask if they were lovers but assumed that they had been. It would have been unrealistic to think otherwise, especially the way things were between Susan and Rick.

"What do you think happened to her, Mike?"

"I was hoping you could tell me. The husband, of course, comes to mind—particularly if he is a jealous fellow. But quite selfishly, I don't want him to be the one. I enjoy his books too much and want him to be able to keep on writing. And as a fellow artist—"

"There was something else." I told him about finding the ledger book and how she had been supplying drugs. He didn't seem surprised, but he listened with such interest that I didn't think he had known anything about it.

"Ah, that would explain what had been bothering her. She hadn't been herself the last couple of weeks—really

119

strung out. She said there was some business she had to wrap up before she went away with me. She even hinted a few times that someone was making it difficult for her to quit, but I thought she was talking about some kind of part-time job she had. I guess I should have asked her. She also said—and this might be important—that she figured on having a nice sum of money of her own to take with us. Said she'd pay her own way while we were abroad—hers and Sara's."

"I don't know. She could have meant blackmail, I suppose, but she could have also saved enough from what she was making, although my sister liked to spend money."

"Tell it to your police friend anyway—maybe it will help. I just hope they get the bastard who killed her. What a waste!"

As though mentioning my "police friend" had summoned him up, Tony picked that moment to come around the side of the church. "I knocked on the door, but nobody answered," he said.

"Do you know each other?" I asked him, and when he answered in the negative, I introduced the two men.

"I've heard a lot about you," Tony said.

"I hate to hear that from a cop," joked Mike.

"No—nothing illegal. Just heard you were a terrific sculptor."

"And local Don Juan," I added.

Mike grinned. "He said that about me?"

I laughed. "Yes, but if you'd like, I'll dispell that rumor. I've found you to be a perfect gentleman."

"Don't bother—I like the sound of 'local Don Juan' better. Care for a cup of coffee, Tony?"

"Got a beer around?"

Tony sat down next to me when Mike went inside to get the drinks. "The lab couldn't come up with anything on your clothes, but then I really didn't expect them to. We're trying to find out about the wig, though. Where it was purchased—things like that."

I told him then what Mike had said about Susan telling him she had to wrap up some business and how she expected to have a nice sum of money. I also told him that my sister had been planning to run off with Mike and take Sara with her.

Mike came back with the drinks, and Tony asked him a few questions, then sat sunk in thought for a while.

"Both things tie in with our theories," Tony finally said. "It's either something to do with the drugs, or it was the jealous husband bit. I wish we could get something more definite on either one. You're just a sitting duck as things stand, Katie, and I don't like it one bit."

"I'm not crazy about it myself," I said vehemently. "Isn't there something I could do to draw whoever it is out in the open? Make myself a target or something?"

"Absolutely not!" said Tony, giving me an exasperated look. "In fact, I'm going to detail a car to watch Rick's house. If he knows it's there, and any outsider can see it sitting there, you should be relatively safe. At least I hope so."

I was about to tell him that wasn't necessary, but on second thought I decided I would feel safer with a police car there.

We talked for a while, and then Tony took off, and I told Mike I should be going also. Before I left, though, he showed me some sketches he had made of Susan. In one, she was sitting on the back of the unicorn, just the way I had been, and I liked it so much that he signed it for me and let me have it.

I took one last look around his wondrous church, then, after promising I would stop by before returning to California, I left for home.

Chapter Twelve

When I got home, I found that it was Mrs. Gurney's afternoon off and that Carol had gone into town to have dinner with her parents. Rick was on the terrace with Sara on his lap. He was patiently dressing one of her dolls while the child chattered away. When I first found I was to be left all alone with Rick, the number-one murder suspect, I felt a moment of pique. Somehow, though, a grown man playing with dolls didn't scare me."

I sat down and watched him with amusement. It was a Barbie doll, which Sara seemed a little young for. He was trying, with great difficulty, to fasten the form-fitting dress. I was about to offer my help when he finally managed the tiny fastenings, and Sara went back into the house to find more clothes for them to play with.

He gave me a wry smile. "I thought that when I got the doll dressed, she would find something for it to do. I believe the doll came with a house and a car and even a boyfriend."

"Actually, the fun is in constantly changing their clothes."

"Did you enjoy your afternoon?"

"Very much. Mike lives in a church he converted, and

it's really spectacular. Have you ever seen any of his work?"

He lighted a cigarette before answering. "I saw one of his shows in New York several years ago and was very impressed. I had heard he had moved up here, but I've never run into him anywhere. Do you happen to know where Susan met him?"

"He didn't say, and I didn't think to ask. By the way, he's quite a fan of yours. He's read all of your books—thinks you might be the best writer in America today."

He raised a brow. "I bet you gave him an argument on that."

"Not at all. I don't think you might be, I think you are." He looked at me in such stunned surprise that I felt myself flush.

"When you said you had read my books, I thought you were just being polite. Anyway, thank you. Now, if the critics just agreed with you . . ."

"What about dinner, Rick? Would you like me to fix something?"

"Would you mind?"

"No, not at all. I'm really not used to being waited on."

"I was going to offer to take you out—"

"Oh, well, then—"

"But I would like to get another hour's writing in before I lose my train of thought."

"Go ahead. I'll keep Sara amused and let you know when dinner's ready."

When Sara came back down, she was carrying an entire wardrobe trunk, miniature-size, filled with outfits for the doll.

"Where's Daddy?"

"He's working."

124

"But he wanted to dress my doll."

"Of course he did, but he had to work. How would you like to go for a swim?" The humidity seemed to be rising for the first time in a couple of days and the thought of a swim really appealed to me.

"Aunt Carol took me to the beach after lunch. I already swam."

"Wouldn't you like to swim again?"

She screwed up her nose and debated the question for a minute, then decided she'd like another swim after all, so we both went upstairs to change.

We didn't spend long in the water, but it was refreshing, and when we got out, I saw that it was clouding up and suspected we were in for another storm.

We were just starting up the steps when I heard someone yell out my name. I turned and saw Johnny coming up the beach.

"Sorry about last night," he said. "I didn't know until too late that Shel thought you were your sister."

"There was no way you could have known." I told him about the trouble afterward, and he let out a curse.

"He can be a mean character when he's crossed. He has a group of kids that act as his minions. But fooling around with a police chief—wow, that's really asking for it."

"Do you have any idea who Susan was getting the drugs from, Johnny?"

"No—that's not something you ask about, you know. But Tony's sharp. I think he'll find out. Of course, there'll be a lot of unhappy people around when he does."

"Including you?"

He laughed. "I'm no serious pothead, Katie. I smoke a little grass now and then—probably equal to what you drink. And I pop some pills at exam time to stay awake, that's all. Don't worry about me being deprived. The stuff's in plentiful supply around Harvard."

I didn't feel I was in any position to lecture him, although I did make attempts occasionally with my high school students. Remembering back to my own student days, there were always girls around with diet pills who would let us have some at exam time. As for marijuana, I had tried it once at a party, and it had put me to sleep. After that I stuck to beer—at least it made me sociable.

Johnny said he was going back to the disco that night and would see if he could find out anything. I told him that if he did, he should speak directly to Tony. I also told him he could spread around the news that I now had police protection in the form of an officer who would be outside the house in a car from now on.

"Did Tony really think that was necessary?"

I remembered I hadn't told him about the fake body on the beach that morning and explained what had happened.

"Hell! I suppose that means I'll be questioned again."

"I don't think anyone suspects you, Johnny. However, if you're missing a blond wig . . ."

He started to look affronted, then realized I was joking and gave a chuckle.

"Listen, Katie, I think I'll start keeping an eye out, too. I'd hate to see anything happen to you."

After Johnny left, we went up to the house, and Sara got into her pajamas while I showered and changed into a white eyelet peasant blouse and wraparound skirt made out of calico. My new image was to be that of kitchen domestic.

I saw no reason why we always had to be so formal and had Sara set the table in the kitchen for a change. She did

it very carefully, almost getting it right, and she seemed
to be having fun helping me. I didn't imagine that my
sister had spent much time in the kitchen, but to be fair,
I wouldn't either if I had Mrs. Gurney.

I will never win any awards with my cooking, but I do
make an exceptional omelet, and combined with the fresh
mushrooms I found in the kitchen, I thought it would do.
I also made a tossed salad and heated up some French
bread spread with garlic butter.

When it was all ready, I sent Sara to fetch her daddy.
They were back in a minute, and I saw Rick's face light
up at what I had prepared.

"This looks sensational. Would you like a bottle of wine
with it?"

"Marvelous," I answered, glad to see that at the moment, at least, we seemed to be enjoying a cease-fire from
our usual bickering.

He complimented me on everything as he ate, and I was
glad I wouldn't have the chance for a repeat performance.
Anything else I cooked wouldn't have matched it.

Sara was falling asleep over her food, and I thought it
was probably due to being at the beach most of the day;
it usually affected me that way. Before we had our coffee,
I suggested to Rick that I take her up to bed. He told me
he would fix the coffee.

When we went to her room, I covered Sara with only
a sheet—it was very warm, and if it did rain and cool off
later, I could put a blanket on her then. She reached her
arms up to me and, when I bent down, she put them
around my neck and pulled my face down, giving me a wet
kiss on the cheek. Then she looked at me, her big eyes
serious.

"You're not my mommy?"

"No, darling, I'm your aunt Katie."

"But I love you."

"I love you too, honey."

"Where's my mommy?"

I didn't know what to say to her—didn't know if she would even understand. Rick spoke from the doorway, and I was saved from answering.

"Your mommy's gone away, Sara," he said to her, leaning down to give her a good-night kiss.

Her lower lip trembled a little. "Is she dead?"

"Do you know what that means, Sara?" he asked her.

"Yes. A boy in my nursery school had a cat that died. And I've seen it on television. Did Mommy die?"

"Yes. Mommy died."

Sara seemed satisfied with the answer. It had probably been confusing for her not knowing what was happening. She said one last thing before closing her eyes. "Aunt Katie? Don't go away."

I was feeling a little tearful when we left the room, but then we heard the first crash of thunder, and we separated and went running around the house, closing all the windows. We were just in time, too, because it really began coming down hard.

Rick asked if I'd like to have our coffee in his study, saying he found it the most pleasant room in the house.

I sat sipping my coffee, feeling very much at peace. I had just fixed dinner for Rick, put his daughter to bed, helped him close up the house against the storm, and I thought to myself how happy I would have been to be his wife and Sara's mother. How ironic it was that the sister he preferred didn't like such a life at all. I must have looked pensive, because he asked me what I was thinking.

"I just don't understand why Susan wasn't happy with all this."

He looked completely relaxed—one leg hooked over the arm of the chair, lazily blowing out smoke and sipping his coffee. "I don't know what to tell you, Kathryn, except that she changed. I think she was too young for marriage and motherhood."

Yes, she had been too young. I was too when I met him. But when you meet the right person, you don't worry about age, because it may never happen again in quite the same way, may never again be perfect. So you take a chance. But for Susan, the chance hadn't worked out.

"How did she change, Rick?"

He leaned his head back and looked beyond me while he spoke. "When I first met her, I found her delightful. She was sweet and rather shy—a calm, happy person. And when she opened up, I found she had a quick, inquiring mind. I liked her—I liked her very much. But she seemed so young and innocent, and she was still in school, and I thought I shouldn't see her again. But then one night she came to the apartment where I was staying. She stood there on my doorstep, crying, saying she had no place to stay. I let her in, and it was very late, so I made up a bed on the couch and then I went to bed. But she didn't stay on the couch.

"I offer no excuses for what happened. I'm only human, and I had been very attracted to her when we met. But I found that she wasn't as innocent as I had thought, and the next morning she seemed to take the whole thing very casually. I saw her a couple of times after that, before I left to come back here. But we weren't in love. Neither of us was serious at all, and I wasn't even attracted to her anymore." He paused and looked at me. "Am I boring you?"

"No. I never knew any of this. She never confided in me."

He went out to the kitchen and came back carrying the coffeepot, pouring us both another cup before sitting down again and resuming where he left off.

"So that's about it. When she showed up here a few weeks later, telling me she was pregnant and her life was ruined and I had to marry her, well . . . I take my responsibilities seriously. And some part of me still hoped that she'd revert to the way she had been when we had first met. But she hated living in New England, she hated being pregnant, and after Sara was born, she soon grew tired of the novelty of having a child. For a very long time, Kathryn, we had been sharing the house like strangers. It was hard on me, and I'm sure it was hard on her."

"I wonder why she didn't leave," I mused, more to myself than to him.

"I think she was waiting for a better alternative. She knew I would fight her over custody of Sara, even though I wouldn't stand a chance in court."

"Thank you for telling me all this, Rick. She never wrote—just sent Christmas cards—so I never knew anything."

"Thank you for listening. And please let me apologize for the way I've behaved toward you since you've been here. I just couldn't believe that you were any different than her, even though everything you said and did belied it. And I can't pretend to have loved your sister when I didn't. So at the risk of making you angry, let me say that I wish it had been you I met first."

130

"You did meet me first. Obviously I didn't make any kind of impression on you."

"You said that when you first came here, but I just can't remember. Were you in one of my seminars?"

"No, those were just for graduate students, and I was only a sophomore. It was during the Christmas holidays. The head of the English department had given a party in your honor, only instead of staying at the party, you took me for a drive down the coast. We ended up in Laguna Beach."

He gave a start and spilled coffee down the front of his shirt. "Oh, God . . ."

I thought he was sick, that something had happened to him, and I stood up and went over to him. "What's the matter, Rick? Are you all right?"

He shook his head, then put his hand over his eyes and sank back into the chair. I went to the kitchen to get a dishcloth to wipe off the coffee he had spilled before it stained his shirt, but when I came back he was standing at the French doors, staring out at the rain. I dropped the cloth on a table and went over to stand beside him.

"Did I say something wrong?"

When he spoke at last, his voice sounded full of regret. "Are you telling me it was you, Kathryn? You whom I drove with to Laguna? But I never knew your name. I called you—"

"Sunshine," I filled in for him. "No, you never asked me my name. It didn't seem important at the time."

"But she seemed to know all about that day."

"Yes, I told her. I was so happy when I got home that day, and she wanted to know why."

"How was I to know you were twins? What a fiasco I

made of things. I think I would have been happier never knowing the truth."

I think *I* would have been happier never knowing, too. He had been attracted to me, and I had never known it. If Susan hadn't died, I would never have seen him again. I was glad I had been able to see him at least once more; perhaps now I would be able to forget him. But I knew that this was pure wishful thinking. The death of my sister would never allow me to forget him.

Carol arrived home and, seeing how subdued we both were, gave us a peculiar look. Rick and Carol chatted awhile about their parents, and I excused myself to go upstairs and put a blanket on Sara. It had become blessedly cooler, and I knew she would need it.

When I came back down, Rick was nowhere to be seen, so I sat down and talked to Carol. She asked me how it had gone with Mike and listened avidly while I described his studio to her.

"Oh, I'd love to see it sometime."

"Go on over. I think he'd be pleased."

She wrinkled her nose. "He'd think I was just another woman chasing after him."

"I'm sure he eats up all that adulation."

"Are you trying a bit of matchmaking, Katie?"

"Not at all. He's not the marrying kind—told me so himself."

"Ummm, a challenge."

"Carol, tell me something."

"Sure, Katie."

"What would Rick have done if Susan had told him she was leaving—going to Europe to live—and taking Sara with her?"

"I shudder to think of it."

"Why?"

"I overheard an argument they had last Christmas. They were in here, and Susan was threatening to leave and take Sara. She said she'd make sure he never saw Sara again. He came storming out of the study, white as a sheet, and I swear he could have easily killed—"

"Killed her?"

"Oh, you know, Katie, that's just a figure of speech. People say it all the time."

"Only she's dead."

"But that was months ago, so I guess they resolved it."

I wasn't so sure. I told her then about my sister's plans to go to Italy with Mike Campbell, and I could see she was upset.

"Did you ask Rick about it?"

"No. I was afraid to."

She turned concerned eyes on me. "Oh, Katie, I'm sorry. I shouldn't have left you alone here with him tonight, not with the way you suspect him. Were you frightened?"

"Of course not. We had a very pleasant and relaxing evening, at least until the end."

"I didn't think things looked good when I came in."

I told her what Rick had told me, and how he had thought Susan was me.

She was almost in tears of sympathy when I finished. "Katie, how sad! What a romantic story. Two doomed lovers forced to live out their lives without each other."

I thought that was putting it on a bit thick. "I thought you weren't a romantic. We are not doomed lovers at all. We're not even lovers."

"Oh, you know what I mean. Well, I for one really

regret the whole thing. I would have loved to have you for a sister-in-law."

"It's too late to cry over it now, Carol. But tell me truthfully what you think Rick would have done if he knew about her running off with Mike."

"I would like to say he would have done nothing, but I'm just not sure. Who knows what will trigger a person. But if he did do it, Katie—not that I think for a minute that he did—I know that you're in no danger from him. Please believe that."

"I know I'm not; he'd have no reason to hurt me."

Carol went to bed then, and I took one of the books down from the shelves so that I'd have something to read in bed. When I turned to leave the room, Rick had entered and was watching me.

"Would you like to take a walk on the beach?" Even as he said it I could hear the rain lashing against the windows. I nodded.

"You don't mind the rain?"

"Not when it's warm out," I answered him, meaning, not when I'm with you, Rick.

He took my hand when we reached the stairs and went ahead of me, leading me down carefully. I could hardly see where we were going except for when the lightning illuminated the way. The storm was wild, but I felt safe and protected with Rick. I don't think it occurred to me once that night to be afraid of being alone with him.

By the time we reached the beach I was completely soaked. My blouse and skirt were plastered against my body, but the rain was warm and felt good on my skin. Rick put his arm around my shoulders, and we started walking along the shore, saying nothing. I leaned against him as we walked, and he tightened his arm. I rested my head on his shoulder. God knows, I knew what I was doing, but I didn't care. I loved the man. Oh, how I loved him!

His silence started to bother me. Walking close to him was lovely, but I wanted more. I wanted to be held in his arms and kissed; I wanted to feel he loved me. That night I wanted the world.

I stopped abruptly and looked up at him, all my longing showing in my eyes for him to see. When he seemed to hesitate, I reached my arms up, put them around his neck, and pulled him toward me. When his lips closed over mine, I closed my eyes and gave myself up to a sea of emotions as powerful and as raging as the sea beyond us. I know he felt as strongly as I, because he pulled me to him so tightly, I could barely breathe, but I didn't care. I would have gladly given up my breath just to be there in his arms.

He could have pulled me down there in the sand if he had wanted to; I wouldn't have stopped him. But his self-control was greater than mine, and he broke off kissing me, loosened his hold on me, and just stood there in the pouring rain, his arms around me, his face rubbing against my hair.

He finally spoke. "Oh, Kathryn. I've relived that day so often, wondering why everything had changed, wondering why it couldn't be recaptured."

I had relived it, too, more times than I could remember. "We're reliving it now," I told him, reaching my face up to him to be kissed again. But instead he let go of me and took my hands in his.

"No, Kathryn. I'm not going to be responsible for your catching pneumonia."

"I'm very healthy." He laughed at that, and it broke the mood.

"Well, then—take pity on an old man." Hand in hand, we started back toward the stairs. "What am I going to do with you, Kathryn? Will you tell me that?"

Keep me, I pleaded silently. Keep me with you—always. His hand seemed to tighten on mine as if he could hear what I was thinking.

He left me at the door to my room, reaching down and placing a chaste kiss on my forehead, his eyes sparkling. "Sleep well," he said as he left me.

I thought I *would* sleep well that night, as my thoughts were all of him before I slept. But my dreams were terrifying. I kept waking up during the night, trying to rid my mind of morbid thoughts, but nothing worked. I kept dreaming the same dream over and over. I would be going down the steps to the beach, and at the bottom would be the effigy of that morning—only in my dream it wasn't an effigy, it was me.

Chapter Thirteen

I felt wrung out the next morning, and even a run on the beach didn't revive me.

"You look terrible. What happened?" Carol remarked when I sat down to breakfast.

I felt Rick's eyes on me, but I didn't glance at him for fear I'd blush. "I just can't get any sleep. Every night I have nightmares and keep waking up. I'd give anything for a good night's sleep."

Rick's voice was gentle. "Paul's coming by for lunch. Have him write you a prescription for something while he's here."

"Maybe I will. I don't like the idea of sleeping pills, but this is getting ridiculous." I looked at him then, and we both smiled, which wasn't lost on Carol.

"What are your plans for today?" he asked us, and I looked at Carol for suggestions.

"Well, we could clean out Susan's room—load up both cars and take the stuff to the church in one trip."

It didn't sound like much fun, but it had to be done, and I didn't see why Carol should be burdened with doing all of it herself.

"Why don't you take some of her clothes, Kathryn?"

Rick was sincere in his offer, I know, but I just couldn't

do it. Once I got back home, I didn't want to be reminded of why I was wearing her clothes every time I got dressed.

"Why don't you move Sara into the room adjoining yours?" I asked Rick. "You two are going to be all alone in this big house, and she's so far down the hall from you, I don't think you'd even hear her if she cried out in the night."

"Good idea," Carol put in.

"Do whatever you want." He seemed to be willing to go along with anything that morning, so I decided to press further.

"Could we fix it up a little for her?" I asked him, thinking of how I'd like to do it.

"And I think she should have a smaller bed," said Carol, mirroring my thoughts. "I had a youth bed when I was a kid, and I'm sure it's still in the attic."

Rick poured himself another cup of coffee and stood up. "You have my permission to do anything you wish. Just don't come in every five minutes with a request while I'm working."

"Sara won't mind, will she?" I asked Carol, afraid the child might be attached to her room.

"Oh, no. She gets little enough attention as it is."

We got to work right after breakfast. We couldn't find any cartons, but Mrs. Gurney gave us dozens of grocery bags, and when we had filled them all with Susan's clothes and carried them out to the cars, we went straight up to the attic.

The youth bed was indeed there, and in addition to that we found a child-size table and four chairs, a rocking horse, and a large blackboard to hang on the wall. It took us awhile, but we finally got it all down and arranged around the hall outside the new bedroom.

"The question is, how do we get that queen-size bed out of there?" I looked at Carol for suggestions.

She was standing in the middle of the room with pursed lips, looking around as though mentally measuring.

"You know, Katie, this is an enormous room. I think we could move Susan's pieces into one corner and still have plenty of room for everything else. And it won't be long before Sara's going to love having that big bed for slumber parties."

We put the table and four chairs in front of the fireplace, the bed coming out from between two windows, and got nails and a hammer to hang up the blackboard. We brought in a small bookcase from Sara's old room to hold some of her toys, and placed some of her games on the table. I sat one of her dolls on the back of the rocking horse. On the large bed we put the child's collection of stuffed animals. We left the dressing table where it was but moved the chaise longue into Rick's bedroom. He had said we could do whatever we wanted, and his room was practically devoid of furniture.

We were very pleased with ourselves when we had finished, and we celebrated our good work with a lemonade provided by a beaming Mrs. Gurney.

After driving the clothes over to the church, Carol went to pick up Sara, and I drove home. Rick and Paul were talking on the terrace, where I joined them, helping myself to some lemonade from a pitcher on the table.

"Rick tells me you've been having trouble sleeping," Paul said to me. "You should have called me. I would have prescribed something for you."

"I've never had any trouble sleeping before," I told him disgustedly, "and I thought it would go away. It's the dreams more than anything. They keep waking me up."

"I'm sure it will go away when you get back home, but I'll write you a prescription for now. You needn't worry about taking the pills—they're not that strong. And you should get some sleep untroubled by dreams." He took a pad out of his pocket and wrote on it, then handed it to me.

I stared at it, frowning. There was something familiar about it.

"What's the matter?" Paul asked me.

"Well, for one thing, I can't read it."

He laughed. "We had a special course in med school on how to write illegibly."

Rick chuckled. "And do the pharmacists get a special class in how to decode it?" We both smiled.

"Of course!"

Carol came in, and we were all in a joking mood throughout lunch.

"When are you returning home?" Paul asked me before he left.

"I don't know. I'm taking my rental car back to Boston tomorrow."

"Is tennis on for Saturday, then?"

"Sure—I'd like that," I answered him, and he said he'd call me and let me know what time he'd pick me up.

When he had gone, Carol flashed me a sly grin. "You're sure making the conquests around here. Tony, Paul, Mike Campbell. Will you tell me your secret?"

"It must be my new deodorant," I countered, and we both broke up laughing. Rick was not amused.

"You're going to Boston tomorrow?" he asked.

"I forgot to mention that." Carol sounded a bit hesitant. "Would it be all right if I brought a guest back for the weekend?"

"Why do you even ask? Your friends are always welcome here."

"Well, this one is a man."

Rick laughed. "It's about time. Who is he?"

As she was telling Rick about Quentin, I suddenly remembered we hadn't shown Sara her new room.

"Have you seen Sara?" I asked Mrs. Gurney, who was clearing off the table.

"She went upstairs for a nap."

Carol broke off talking to Rick, looked at me in horror, and we both dashed upstairs.

Sara looked very woebegone in her bed stripped of linens. She smiled at us tremulously. "My toys are all gone."

Carol and I both could have wept. I lifted up Sara and carried her into her new room, and the look on the child's face when I put her down was worth a hundred times the work we had done.

She went right to the rocking horse and patted it on the head. She sat down in every one of the four chairs around the table, and climbed into the youth bed, settling down with an ecstatic smile on her face.

"Do you like it?" Carol asked her.

"I love it," she said and closed her eyes.

Carol and I drove into town that afternoon and picked up a few additional things for Sara's room. Neither one of us felt ambitious enough to wallpaper, but we found some charming framed prints of nursery-rhyme characters to hang on the walls and bought a quilt for her bed with cloth lambs embroidered on it. I wanted to buy Sara something special to remember me by, and in one of the department stores I found a delicate gold chain with a tiny gold heart for her to wear around her neck.

When we got home, Sara had woken up and watched

with delight as we hung the pictures and put the new quilt on her bed.

When I fastened the gold chain around her neck, she ran to see herself in the mirror.

"Pretty . . ." she said over and over, then ran to give me a hug. "I wish you were my mommy," she said.

I looked at Carol.

"You can buy that kid with gold," she joked, and we both laughed a bit shakily.

When we got downstairs, Tony was there talking to Rick, and we joined them.

Tony reached down, picked up a scrap of paper under his chair, and looked at it. "What's this—someone's prescription?"

I gave a disgusted sigh. "I went to town and forgot all about it. Paul wrote me a prescription because I've been having trouble sleeping."

He looked at it again. "Why don't I have my stakeout have it filled for you?"

"That's too much trouble," I protested.

"He won't think so," Tony disagreed. "That way he can get himself some ice cream and take a little break. It's not exactly exciting out there, you know."

"Well, if you put it that way . . ."

He was back in a few minutes. "I just stopped by to see how you were doing," Tony said to me, sitting back down.

Sara came running out of the house and climbed into Rick's lap. "Look, Daddy. Look what Auntie Katie gave to me." The heart was duly admired, and Rick gave me a warm smile.

"I'm doing fine," I told Tony. "Nothing exciting at all has happened today."

"Well, don't sound disappointed." He laughed.

142

Paul came over to dinner that night, and afterward Carol and I watched an old movie on TV while the men talked in Rick's study. I was dozing on the couch when Paul came in to say good night.

"You don't look like you require sleeping pills," he joked. "What you need, young lady, is a good run on the beach."

"Is that a challenge, Doctor?"

"You can take it as such. I bet you think we're not in as good shape here as you health-conscious Californians."

"That's a challenge I can't resist," I told him, getting up. "Want to join us, Carol?"

"Not me." She laughed. "I'll admit to being in bad shape—and I'm going to stay that way."

The moon was full, and we could see our way clearly going down the steps and onto the beach. I took off my shoes and traced a starting line on the sand with my toe.

"Is this going to be a race?" Paul asked.

"Yes, it is. To that rock formation down there and back. And if you can manage that, we'll try something longer."

"Think I'm not up to it, don't you?"

I looked him over slowly. "Well, you're probably in good shape from tennis, but that's a whole different set of muscles."

"We'll see," he muttered, assuming a runner's stance at the starting line.

He was fast enough, and I only beat him by a couple of seconds, but he was so winded from the exertion that he collapsed on the sand after the first run.

I crouched down beside him. "Thought you were so smart challenging me, didn't you?" I teased him. I saw an evil gleam in his eyes just before he reached out and pulled me half on top of him and gave me a resounding kiss. At least I think that's what you'd call it—it was playful, anyway. But then it turned less playful and more serious, and I pulled away, assuming a mock indignant look.

"How dare you, Doctor?"

"Very easily—you were tempting me, Kathryn."

"I was not!"

"Ah, Kathryn, would you laugh at me if I said I was falling in love with you?"

"Yes, I would."

"I was afraid you'd say that. But seriously, my girl, you're the first female I've felt the slightest desire for in a very long time."

"I'm really having trouble seeing myself as a femme fatale, Paul."

"I still detect a little bit of an inferiority complex, Kathryn. Why can't you believe you're a desirable woman? Tony Greco certainly thinks so. And I'm sure Rick would if you didn't so vividly remind him of Susan."

That showed he wasn't as perceptive as he thought. The conversation was getting a bit sticky, so I got up, preparing to go back to the house.

Paul rose, too, and took my hand. "Okay—I'm sorry I came on so strong so soon. But we can be friends, can't we?"

I squeezed his hand.

"But don't think I'm going to stop trying," he added. "It's really been a long time since I've felt this way; I had almost forgotten what it was like."

I didn't answer him. I didn't want to encourage him, and I just didn't know him well enough to have any kind of feelings for him, but I was glad of his friendship.

Unfortunately Rick saw us coming into the house hand

in hand and probably looking somewhat bedraggled from the run. He was about to say something, and I'm sure it wouldn't have been complimentary, when Paul spoke up.

"Just a run on the beach, Rick—perfectly innocent, I assure you."

Rick just gave us a disbelieving look and disappeared into his study.

Paul looked at me and shrugged. "I'll explain to him that it was perfectly innocent—unfortunately."

"Don't worry about it, Paul. I'm sure he knows it was innocent."

"Well, don't forget to take a pill tonight, Kathryn. Pleasant dreams."

I went upstairs, feeling dismay at Rick's reaction. He just couldn't believe that I was on the beach kissing him one night and then doing the same thing with Paul the next. Except that it was something my sister would have done. I hoped very much that the closeness we had begun to build hadn't been shattered.

I got ready for bed and took one of the sleeping pills, hopeful of finally getting a night of unbroken sleep.

Sara's screams awakened me at about 4:00 A.M., and I struggled to consciousness, trying to fight the effects of the pill, but it was several minutes before I was able to get out of bed and into my robe. I stumbled down the hall to Sara's room. The lights were on, and Carol and Rick were already there, Rick holding Sara and comforting her.

"What happened?" I asked Carol.

"Someone was searching Sara's room and woke her up."

I felt very unsteady on my legs and sat down on the edge of Sara's bed. "Why would someone want to search Sara's room?" I asked, my mind not functioning very clearly.

Carol looked at Rick before answering me. "Up until today it was Susan's room. I guess we should have left it that way—it's sure a shambles now, and I wouldn't have had Sara frightened for anything."

I looked around. Drawers had been dumped on the floor, their contents strewn. The bedding, along with the stuffed animals, had been pulled off Susan's bed, and it looked as though the intruder had looked under the mattress, as it was askew. Even the small bookcase filled with toys that we had brought from Sara's room had been turned over.

I suddenly realized it was all my fault that someone had come in here and frightened Sara. And this time it wasn't Rick's doing, that I was certain of. Not only was I sure that he wouldn't have frightened his daughter, but I knew it was someone looking for the ledger book. If I hadn't kept quiet about having found it, and turned it over to Tony, this wouldn't have happened.

Tears started to run down my face. "Please, someone call Tony. There could be fingerprints or something."

Carol took Sara from Rick's arms. "I'll take her to my room for the rest of the night, Rick. You call Tony."

"We better not touch anything in here," Rick said to me. "Do you want to go downstairs with me and wait for Tony, or would you rather go back to bed? You look terrible."

I stood up and started to sway on my feet. "It's the sleeping pill I took," I explained to him as he grabbed my arm and steadied me. "I'm not used to them."

He helped me down the stairs to his study, where he deposited me in a chair before making the phone call. From what I could gather, the police would be right over. He then went to make some coffee.

146

When he returned, he poured me some coffee and held the mug while I took a sip. "This is going to wake me up," I muttered.

"Good. Tony will probably want to question us."

"But I don't know anything—except that it was all my fault."

"No, Kathryn, it wasn't all your fault. I gave you permission to move Sara's things into that room, and Carol helped you. We're all at fault in this."

I shook my head. "No, that wasn't what I meant. If I had told everyone I had already found it, the room probably wouldn't have been searched."

"What did you find?"

The coffee was helping to clear my head, and I decided I'd better not say anything further until Tony arrived. "Never mind—it probably doesn't matter now."

The doorbell rang and moments later Rick ushered in Tony, looking about as sleepy as I felt, and a young officer in uniform.

"I just don't understand it," Tony was saying to Rick. "Jack's been out in front all night and didn't see anyone entering or leaving."

"It was no one in this house, Tony," Rick told him, a touch of anger in his voice.

Tony and I exchanged glances. "I know, Rick, this time it was definitely drug-related, but how the hell did he get in and out without my man spotting him?"

"It was my fault, Tony," I said. "If I had told everyone about finding the—what I gave you, this wouldn't have happened."

"No, you're wrong, Katie. The right person wouldn't necessarily have heard. This could have been anyone."

The men from the lab arrived then to dust the room for fingerprints, and Tony took them upstairs. I don't know what happened after that. I must have fallen asleep in the chair, because the next thing I remember, Rick was tucking me in my bed and telling me to get some more sleep. But all of that is very vague, particularly the part where he kissed me good night.

Chapter Fourteen

Despite what had happened the night before, or rather in the early morning, I awoke refreshed with no memory of bad dreams.

I decided to forego my run, and instead took a leisurely bath and dressed with care in a dress of stretch terry cloth in a luscious shade of pimiento. With it I wore the white sandals and pulled my hair back with two combs.

Carol had wanted to get an early start, but I found she wasn't down yet, and I headed for the kitchen to see if I could beg a cup of coffee from Mrs. Gurney.

"I heard you had a little trouble last night," she said to me.

"Yes. Do you know how Sara is this morning?"

"Oh, the little one has forgotten all about it already—probably thinks it was all a dream. She was driven off to nursery school by her father, chatting away as though nothing had happened."

"Thank goodness for that," I said, feeling much relieved to hear it.

"My, you look lovely in that color," she said to me approvingly, and I must have looked surprised, because she went on. "Altogether you're a lovely young lady, and

I'm sorry if I was less than welcoming when you first arrived."

"Well, thank you, but it's all right—I understood." She already had a cup of coffee poured for me, and I sat down at the kitchen table to drink it.

"No, it's not all right. People have a right to be judged on their own merits, and I was unfair to you. And the way you've been with little Sara—so loving and caring. Well, I told Mr. Allison, and I'll tell you—I'll be sorry to see you go."

"Thank you, Mrs. Gurney, that's nice to hear. And don't think I'm going to lose touch with Sara. I plan on coming back to visit her from time to time."

I looked up then and saw Rick standing in the doorway and wondered how much he had overheard. "I'm glad to hear Sara's okay this morning," I told him.

"Yes, she was fine. She didn't seem to even remember anything happening."

"Well, tell your lazy sister to get a move on," I said to him, "while Mrs. Gurney and I get breakfast on the table."

It wasn't the usual eggs that morning. Mrs. Gurney had outdone herself with thin, light, delicious pancakes and fat little sausages, and if I admitted to having three helpings, I wouldn't be exaggerating.

"I expect they still serve food in Boston," Rick said dryly, causing me to choke on my last bite.

"How are you doing the trip, Carol? Are you taking both cars and having Kathryn follow you in?"

Carol shook her head and hastily swallowed the last of her pancakes. "No, we'll drive in with Katie's car, call Quentin from the airport, and he'll drive us back. Don't expect us for dinner. We'll show Katie a little of Boston and stop for something on the way back."

Rick walked us out to the car when we left. "You sure you don't want to take both cars?" he asked his sister. "That way you won't be stuck if something happens to Quentin."

"Nothing will happen to Quentin," Carol assured him, getting into the passenger seat.

I put on my sunglasses and started up the car.

"Fasten your seat belt," Rick ordered Carol, and she gave him an exasperated look.

"Will you quit fussing?"

I pulled out of the driveway onto the road and headed for town to pick up the highway.

"Would you rather I drove or gave you directions?" Carol asked me.

"I'd rather drive—I miss it. And I'm pretty sure I remember the way."

I was driving about forty-five or fifty when I hit a sharp curve and braked to slow down. Only there were no brakes —my foot went right to the floor, and the car screeched around the curve on two wheels.

Carol started to say something about California drivers, but then saw the look on my face. "What is it, Katie?"

My stomach muscles were tightening, and I thought I was going to be sick. "The brakes are gone."

Her face mirrored my horror. "My God, what'll we do?"

A smooth stretch of road was in front of us, and I knew there was no immediate danger. I had long ago decided that if this ever happened to a car I was driving, I would shift into reverse and simply drop the transmission if need be, but in this case I didn't think such a drastic measure was called for.

I pulled up the emergency brake, but it only slowed us down slightly. The road sloped somewhat downhill and even though I was no longer accelerating, we were still maintaining about forty-five MPH.

I looked to the right and saw a grassy verge sloping down from the road, but not too steeply. I glanced over to see if Carol had indeed fastened her seat belt. She had, so I drove straight off the road and onto the grass.

The car gradually lost speed and came to rest at the bottom, slightly tipped to one side.

Carol managed a shaky smile as she unfastened her seat belt. "So much for rented cars."

I took a few deep breaths to try to calm myself, then got out and leaned against the side of the car.

Carol joined me. "Are you all right, Katie?"

"There was nothing wrong with this car," I said very quietly. "Someone fixed the brakes."

Her eyes were wide. "What do you mean?"

"I mean that someone did whatever one does to brakes to make them not work. I imagine the brake fluid has been drained."

"Oh, my God, Katie. But who?"

"Well, Carol, I think it was your brother," I said despondently.

"Oh, no! But he wouldn't do anything to hurt me."

"Just think about it a minute, Carol. He had assumed, I believe, that we were taking two cars. When he found out differently, he suggested we take two. And when that didn't work, he made sure you fastened your seat belt. He wasn't trying to kill me, Carol. He knows this road, knows it wouldn't be that dangerous. It was just another attempt to scare me off."

"I don't know, Katie; I don't know what to believe anymore."

"We're not far from town. Let's start walking. Does the gas station there have a tow truck?"

"I'm sure they do. But we're closer to home. Why don't we call from there?"

"I don't feel up to facing Rick right now, do you mind?" I was being rude to Carol, who had done nothing to deserve it, but I felt a growing anger I couldn't control.

We got our purses out of the car and started to walk to town. There was no sidewalk, and the road was rough. We were both wearing heels, which slowed us down considerably, and I wished I had worn pants. It was getting very warm already, and my perspiring face felt covered by a layer of dust.

Inside, I felt devoid of any feelings except anger. How could someone who was so sweet and loving to me the day before do such a sick and vicious thing? I had begun to think he cared about me. Even though some things pointed to him as Susan's killer, some part of me had never really believed it. But no more. I was not such a masochist as to continue loving someone who was deliberately trying to scare me off, to say nothing of having killed Susan. Nothing made any sense. The only rational explanation I could come up with was that Rick had some kind of dual personality that allowed him to behave one way one day and completely opposite the next.

We completed the walk to town in silence. The gas station had a tow truck and immediately dispatched it to where we had left the car.

"What do you want to do now, Katie? I guess we better

forget about Boston." Carol looked as though she expected me to be angry with her, and I softened toward her.

"No, let's go on, Carol. I have no desire to return to the house. It shouldn't take long for them to fix the car."

We waited in the station's office, and I used the phone to call Tony. I told him briefly what had happened, and he said he'd be right over.

After my call, Carol called Quentin to tell him we'd be arriving a little later than anticipated.

The tow truck pulled in right in front of Tony. I saw him conferring with the station manager, then they both looked under the hood.

I went outside and stood beside Tony, and he put a reassuring arm around my shoulders.

"Was the brake fluid removed?" I asked the manager.

"Sure looks that way. I'll have it all fixed up for you in no time."

Tony led me over to his car, and I got inside with him and told him everything that had happened that morning.

"Did anyone else know you were going to Boston?"

I shook my head.

"It sure looks as though Rick's our man," he commented, "but unless he confesses, I doubt we'll ever be able to pin it on him. So my advice to you, Katie, is to return to California and get any ideas of revenge out of your mind."

I thought of leaving Sara there alone with him, but I didn't believe for a moment that he would harm her. What he had done had probably been motivated by his love for her more than anything else.

I nodded. "We're driving into Boston now. I'll reserve a flight back on Sunday." I was reaching for the door handle when he detained me.

"I think we have a lead on the drug supplier. We're

checking it out now, doing some investigating. Anyway, I'll let you know if anything breaks. But your sister's death—well, I'm sure that was a personal motive."

"Thanks, Tony." He was a good man, and I regretted not being able to feel anything more than friendship for him, as I knew he was interested.

The car was ready to go, and I paid the station manager with one of my credit cards. He knew it was a rental and suggested I present the rental agency with the bill, but since it had been deliberate, I didn't feel it was ethical to make them pay for it.

I used the washroom to clean some of the dust off my face and arms, then Carol and I got back in the car. We drove for a while in silence, and when it began to be uncomfortable not talking, I told her of my plans to return to California on Sunday.

She seemed relieved that I had spoken first. "Quentin and I will drive you to the airport. And, Katie, we'll make sure you're not alone with Rick until you leave."

"I won't be at the house much, anyway. I'm playing tennis with Paul tomorrow."

I was feeling depressed and couldn't shake it off. I had accomplished very little on my trip, except for becoming acquainted with my niece. And that might prove not to have been in the child's best interests. First her mother had vanished from her life, and soon I was to do the same.

The rest of the drive was uneventful, and I turned in the car at the agency while Carol telephoned Quentin. The huge bill I was running up on my credit card would preclude my taking any other trips that summer, but I had no wish now to do anything but just stay home.

Carol came back, saying we had about forty minutes before Quentin would arrive, so we went over to the airlines counter and I made a reservation for Sunday afternoon. Then we went into the airport coffee shop and ordered sandwiches.

Carol talked to me about Quentin while we waited. She had met him several months before at a concert given by the Boston Symphony Orchestra. They had been seated next to each other, both had been alone, and they had struck up a conversation during intermission. They had found they had mutual friends, similar interests, and the same dry sense of humor.

"He's really quite impossible," she related with a fond smile. "He's never on time, sometimes completely forgets a date, and we argue about everything. But when we're together, he makes me feel more alive than I've ever felt. I come from a very low-key, introspective family, and he's a complete extrovert, full of nervous energy. Oh, well, you'll soon see for yourself."

"How do you feel about him?" I asked, genuinely interested.

"I can't figure that out, actually. I've gone out with other men since I've met him, but they all seem boring next to Quentin. But I don't feel like I've been struck by lightning, either."

I hope I didn't show my amazement when I had my first look at Quentin towering over our table. He wasn't much over six feet but appeared taller because of his extreme thinness and a head of fuzzy blondish hair, which added several inches. He had a large nose, small but piercing green eyes, and a funny, crooked smile.

He shook my hand, sat down with us briefly, then hustled us out to his car, all the while talking a mile a minute. His rate of speed combined with his Boston accent caused me to grasp only about a third of what he said, but I gathered it was mostly about what had been happening in the city during Carol's absence.

Because of our delay in getting there, and in order to avoid the Friday night exodus of cars heading for the seashore, we decided to just stop by Carol's apartment briefly so that she could pick up some things she needed, before heading back to Cauley.

Quentin gave me a quick tour by car of the city. I heard such familiar names as Bunker Hill, Paul Revere's house, Boston Common, and others being shouted out with gusto from the front seat, but when I'd look out the back window, I couldn't tell what I was supposed to be looking at.

I got glimpses of Harvard as we drove through Cambridge to Carol's apartment, and I found the area full of charm.

She had a tiny one-bedroom apartment on the first floor of a brownstone. It had its own walled-in garden in the back, and Quentin made himself at home in a hammock strung out between the garden's one tree and the brick wall. I looked around the apartment while Carol packed a few clothes and books she wanted. What struck me most about her place was that it had a feeling of permanence. It was a home, unlike my apartment in California, which resembled a cross between a dormitory and a motel suite. We had taped a few travel posters to the walls but had never gotten around to hanging pictures. And instead of real beds, we were still sleeping on mattresses and box springs placed on the floor.

Many plants in baskets were placed near the windows, and they didn't appear to be doing well. "Do you want me to water your plants for you?" I called out to her.

"Oh, would you, Katie? There's a watering can in the kitchen."

I found her red watering can and gave the plants a good soaking along with a little advice. Carol came in, heard me talking to her plants, and burst out laughing. "You're marvelous at that! I always feel silly talking out loud to inanimate objects."

"Shame on you, Carol—plants aren't inanimate!"

"I'm becoming an inanimate object out here all alone," Quentin's voice was heard from the yard. "And if you have any iced tea, Carol . . ."

She made up a pitcher of iced tea while I finished watering the plants, and then we sat out in the yard, and I listened while they got caught up with each other.

To see them together one would think them an unlikely couple, he so tall and rangy and she rather tiny and delicate-looking. But their minds were attuned, their attitudes in harmony, and I hoped that Carol wouldn't wait for lightning to strike. I thought it already had and she just didn't realize it.

We left soon to beat the rush-hour traffic, but even so, the roads leading out of Boston were crowded, and we crawled along, not making any time at all. It was hot in the car, and Quentin didn't have air conditioning, but once we got beyond the city it became more pleasant.

"Have you seen anything of Cape Ann while you've been here?" Quentin asked me.

Carol explained to him that I had come for my sister's funeral, and that necessitated more explanations as Quentin had an avid curiosity about the whole affair and asked countless questions.

"But you can't believe Rick Allison is a murderer!" He turned around and gave me a disbelieving look. "Why, he writes marvelous books—absolutely marvelous. I've been *dying* to meet him. I was looking forward to having him for a brother-in-law, but a *murderer?*"

It was Carol's turn to give him a questioning look. "Brother-in-law? This is the first I've heard of our getting married."

"Well, we won't be unless we get this thing solved."

"Are you implying, Quentin, that you'd marry me just to have a famous writer for an in-law?" She looked back at me and shook her head in wonder.

"It's a definite asset," he told her seriously, then laughed at her look of outrage. "I'm joking, I'm joking! Have your lost your sense of humor?"

She moved closer to him in the front seat. "What you said before, Quentin, about whether Katie's been anywhere since she's been here. Why don't we take her to Gloucester for a seafood dinner and then drive over to Rockport and walk around the shops for a while?"

"Okay with me, luv," he agreed.

I, of course, was also agreeable—anything to prolong returning to the house and having to see Rick again. I wondered what he was thinking then, whether he had heard of our mishap from Tony or was just left wondering what had happened to us. What a shock it must have been for him when he learned that Carol was driving with me. I really wasn't afraid of him. I just felt great pity. His world seemed to be crumbling around him, and whether he was caught or not, his sensitivity was such that I was sure his life from then on would be adversely affected by what he had done. I felt that my sister's death had probably been an accident. She had no doubt taunted him about running off with Mike and taking Sara along, and he had hit out at her in anger. Then, to protect his reputation, or maybe to protect Sara and his family, he had

159

started to cover it up with a series of lies until he was stuck in such a maze of deception that he couldn't extricate himself without looking very bad. If this was what had happened, then I thought I could live with it. At least it diminished my opinion of him to the extent that I thought in time I would be able to get over him and carry on with my life, perhaps with someone else. I envied Quentin and Carol their easy familiarity in the front seat. I had never had that with a man. I think I could have with Rick if circumstances had been different.

I adored Gloucester. It had nothing cute or contrived about it, but looked truly like an authentic seaport. We ate in an elegantly simple restaurant that jutted out over the water, and the food was delicious. Quentin wouldn't let up playing detective all through dinner. He wanted to know every detail of what had happened since I had arrived. With his vivid imagination he built up a case against just about anyone I mentioned—even supposing that Tony Greco had had an illicit affair with my sister and was not "bungling" the case in an attempt to have it remain unsolved. But try as he might to absolve Rick, it just didn't work. Everything pointed to him, and even Quentin finally admitted as much.

"Not that I'm convinced Rick did it, mind you," he assured us. "I'll want to question him at length. It seems to me that's what no one has done—question the prime suspect."

As we were leaving the restaurant I caught sight of Paul and a very beautiful woman dining together in a secluded corner. They were sitting very close together, and as I watched, he leaned over and kissed her. So I was the first female he had felt any desire for in a long time, was I? *Men,* I thought to myself; *you can't trust any of them.*

160

Rockport was definitely a tourist attraction. Throngs of people strolled down the sidewalks lined with shops, and it took us almost an hour just to find a parking space.

Carol and I wanted to go in every shop we passed; Quentin wanted to hurry us along so he could meet Rick. We compromised by only going into shops that had something satisfying to offer Quentin's taste buds. We got a large bag of saltwater taffy and each had a chocolate ice-cream cone.

When we had traversed the full length of the street and there was no longer an excuse not to go home, Quentin finally managed to get us back to his car. It was after eleven by then, and I hoped that perhaps Rick had already gone to bed.

When we pulled into the driveway, the downstairs lights were on, and Rick met us at the door. I avoided looking at him altogether and saw that Carol was a bit nervous. I didn't know whether her nervousness was a result of bringing Quentin home to meet her brother or because of the incident that morning, but I hoped it was the former. I didn't want to be the cause of a wedge between a very close brother/sister relationship.

I needn't have worried about what to say. Quentin was his usual garrulous self from the moment we stepped in the door. Rick had made a pot of coffee, and I found myself sitting around the kitchen table, having a cup with the others.

Quentin didn't know the meaning of the word tact. "I don't care what the girls say," he announced to Rick almost immediately. "I don't believe for a minute you fixed those brakes."

It's odd that a remark like that would have the effect on me of wanting to sink under the table out of sight. I had nothing to feel guilty about—*I* was the injured party—and yet such outspokenness made me uncomfortable. *I* felt guilty at the implied accusation. I couldn't account for how I felt, but I could see that Carol felt exactly the same. Her brother had done something that could conceivably have resulted in her injury, yet she would have been embarrassed to mention it.

Conversely, Rick seemed not at all dismayed by the remark. His eyes held a hint of humor as he looked from Carol to me, then back at Quentin.

"I see I have a champion."

"Damn right, man, and I say we should get to the bottom of things. All it should take is a logical mind—and I know you've got one of those. Clear as anything in those books you write. And I've got one, too; Carol can testify to that."

"What do you suggest?" Rick asked him equably.

"I want to hear your side of it. All I've heard so far is pure conjecture. It seems to me that everyone's been pussyfooting around you, never asking you a straight question. That's what I intend to do—ask you some straight questions. And I don't care if it takes all night."

Carol and I exchanged glances. I didn't know how she felt, but as far as I was concerned, it had gone a lot further than just conjecture. I wasn't about to stay up all night just to hear Rick try to exonerate himself. He hadn't defended himself about the brakes and even seemed to take it lightly. I felt the less I saw of him before I left, the better, and so I excused myself, mentioning the tennis game the following day.

Rick looked over at me. "Sorry. I forgot to tell you. Paul called and said he'd pick you up around noon. Said to tell you to dress for tennis but bring a bathing suit. The country club has a pool, and he thought you might like to go for a swim after your game." There seemed to be a special light in his eyes when he talked to me; the light in mine, I felt, had gone.

"Who's Paul?" Quentin asked Carol.

"An old friend—he went to school with Rick."

"Sounds good to me. Why don't we join them?"

Carol shrugged helplessly. "It's all right with me. In that case, though, I'm going to bed, too. It's been a long day."

Carol and I went upstairs, and I stopped by her room to talk for a minute. "I think he's fantastic, Carol. Are you going to marry him?"

"Don't ask me—he seems to make all the decisions on his own."

I laughed. "I noticed. But I liked that about him. He has such a positive attitude, like he can't fail at anything."

"I know. He was like that from the beginning. He just sort of took over my life. I hope you don't mind his just inviting us along with you and Paul tomorrow."

"No, I'm glad. It'll be more fun. I really don't know Paul very well, but I could hardly refuse a tennis game. And thanks to him I got a good night's sleep last night."

"Oh, Paul's great. He was always like another older brother to me when I was growing up. For a short time, when I was in college, we even dated. But it was no good. He just really did seem like a brother."

"Unlike Quentin?"

"Unlike Quentin, even though they are about the same age. I guess it was just that I grew up with Paul always around the house."

We talked a little longer, but we were both tired, so I finally went to my room. I was so tired, in fact, that I debated whether or not I needed a sleeping pill. I finally took one just to dispel any dreams. I knew what I would dream that night if I didn't take one. I would dream about the brakes going out and Carol and I plunging over a cliff. I didn't want to dream that. I suddenly wanted my smooth stretch of beach at home. It might not be as beautiful as this coastline, but it was a lot safer.

Chapter Fifteen

I woke up slowly the next morning, feeling a little groggy from the sleeping pill. It was early, and I remained in bed awhile, seeing if I could fall back to sleep, but I finally got up and went over to the window. It was a perfect day. The blue sky was cloudless. It was warm but the humidity seemed low, and a nice breeze was coming in the window. It would be my last day there, and I prayed that it would be an uneventful one. I would make sure Rick knew I was returning home the next day, so there would be no need for him to make any more attempts to scare me off.

I went into the bathroom and took a shower, washing my hair at the same time. I dried it, then fastened it in pigtails with rubber bands to keep it out of my eyes when I played tennis.

I dressed in Carol's navy-blue shorts and a T-shirt, and wore my running shoes in lieu of tennis sneakers, which I didn't have with me. I took a look at myself in the mirror and saw that I looked about twelve.

It was still early, so I packed some of my clothes, then thought about calling Cindy to let her know I was coming home. It was an ungodly hour to call California, but probably the only time I'd catch her at home on a Saturday.

I called collect and heard her sleepy voice accepting the call.

"Sorry about the hour, Cindy."

"Katie? I've been worried about you. How's it going?"

"It would take too long to tell you, and I don't want to run up the phone bill. Anyway, I'll be back tomorrow. Can you pick me up?"

"Sure—let me get a pencil."

I gave her the flight number and arrival time, then told her to go back to sleep.

I went downstairs quietly. No one seemed to be up yet, and I wondered how late Quentin and Rick had stayed up talking. Mrs. Gurney was sitting at the kitchen table, drinking coffee and reading the newspaper, so I poured myself a cup and joined her.

She asked me if Carol's young man had arrived, and I told her yes, and that he and Rick had probably stayed up pretty late talking.

I took a section of her paper and glanced at it as we talked. The world could have gone to war that week and I wouldn't have known it, I realized. I hadn't seen a newspaper or watched the news on TV since I'd been there.

I was on my second cup of coffee when Sara came in, dressed except for her shoes, which she carried by the laces. I lifted her onto the counter and put them on for her.

"You running on the beach, Auntie Katie?"

"No, not today." It wasn't a bad idea, but then I'd have to shower and wash my hair again, and I wasn't feeling that ambitious.

Mrs. Gurney fixed Sara's breakfast, but I wasn't hungry yet and decided to wait for the others to get up. I sat with Sara while she ate and stole a piece of her toast.

"I'm going back to California tomorrow, Mrs. Gurney." I was waiting to see Sara's reaction to the news, but she didn't seem upset as I had feared.

"You going home?" she asked me matter-of-factly.

"Yes, honey. But I'll come back and see you."

She looked doubtful at that, and I started to feel like I was abandoning her. "And when you get older, Sara, you can come visit me in California."

Mrs. Gurney shook her head and smiled. "She doesn't understand you now, but she'll appreciate your keeping in touch as she gets older."

Quentin was the next to find his way to the kitchen. He flirted with a flustered but pleased Mrs. Gurney and took an enchanted Sara for a ride on his shoulders down to the beach. I was sure there was no one beyond his capacities to charm.

The telephone rang, and Mrs. Gurney said it was for me. I thought it might be Paul or Tony and was surprised when Johnny Fowler announced himself.

"Katie, I found out some stuff I think you should pass along to the police chief."

"What is it, Johnny?"

"Well, I was at the disco last night, and I talked to a few of the guys. Then Shel let slip that he had a good idea who your sister was fronting for. Can we meet and talk?"

"Johnny, call Tony and tell him everything you know."

"Ah, Katie, couldn't you do that?"

"Don't be such a chicken. He's not going to arrest you for anything. He's going to want to question you, anyway."

"But don't you want to know what I found out?"

"Not really. I'm going home tomorrow, and I really don't care about the drug part of it anymore."

167

"You sound depressed, Katie."

"Well, I guess I am a little. It hasn't been a great week."

"Listen, do you want some pills?"

"No, Johnny, I do not want any pills! I'll be fine when I get home."

"Well, have a good trip, Katie, and I hope I see you again sometime."

"Thanks, Johnny—me too."

When I got off the phone, I saw that Carol and Rick were out on the terrace. I joined them.

Carol and I took one look at each other and laughed. We were dressed almost identically with our hair in pigtails.

"Where's Quentin?" she asked me.

"Down on the beach with Sara. And, Carol, that man of yours could charm a snake."

She chuckled. "Tell me about it!"

Rick looked over at me. "Kathryn, I was just talking to Carol about the accident with the car yesterday, and I wanted—"

"Forget it," I interrupted him. "I'm going home tomorrow, and it just doesn't matter anymore."

He looked startled at my news and seemed about to say something else, but Quentin and Sara appeared at the top of the steps then and after that, breakfast was served. As usual, Quentin both directed and dominated the conversation.

Sara appeared entranced with Quentin. She stayed by his side while he ate breakfast, and when he was finished, she climbed up on his lap.

"Are you going to be my niece, Sara?" he asked her, and she nodded her head enthusiastically.

Rick turned to Carol. "You're getting married?"

"Don't ask me, I'm never told anything. Ask the expert over there."

Quentin grinned his crooked grin. "We'll see—I'm thinking about it. Sara is a plus in your favor, of course."

Carol looked like she could have kicked him, and I had to laugh.

Mrs. Gurney yelled out the window that Gus Tornetta was on the phone for Rick.

"My agent—and I'm behind on my book," Rick explained as he excused himself.

"Well, what did you find out last night?" Carol asked Quentin as soon as Rick was out of earshot.

"Your brother is a man of integrity."

"What else?"

"That says it all," Quentin replied cryptically and wouldn't say another word on the subject.

Paul arrived shortly before noon and was introduced to Quentin.

"We've invited ourselves along for tennis," Quentin informed him.

Carol was heard to mutter, "What do you mean, 'we'?"

"Great," said Paul. "Doubles are even better. I hope you're a good player, Kathryn, because I know Carol is. I taught her."

"I haven't played for a while," I admitted.

"Don't worry about it—Quentin's lousy," Carol said, then ducked when Quentin tried to cuff her playfully.

Carol went out to the garage to find us all tennis rackets, and Paul asked Rick if he'd like to join us. I realized it was kind of rude of us to all go off and have a good time and leave him all alone, but he pleaded work.

We drove off in Paul's car and were at the club in about twenty minutes. There was a long, low clubhouse complete with dining room, bar, and locker rooms. In addition to the tennis courts and pool, there was also an eighteen-hole golf course and a racquetball court.

We sat around in deck chairs, drinking while waiting for a court to open up. Paul had been at Harvard Medical School when Quentin was an undergraduate there, and they reminisced about their college days.

"He is starting to give me a pain," Carol said to me in an undertone. "I wanted everyone to like him, but they don't have to fall all over themselves in their enthusiasm."

"He seems to evoke a strong response in people," I said, not bothering to lower my voice as Quentin was expounding on something rather loudly at the moment.

"Ummm—you should see him with his students. The boys try to emulate him, and the girls try to seduce him."

I couldn't help laughing at that, although Carol didn't seem to share my mirth. Paul looked over and winked at me, then drew his attention back to Quentin.

A court opened up, and we agreed to play three sets of doubles. I was a bit rusty but didn't do too badly. Paul and Carol were both excellent players. I couldn't tell about Quentin, but he tipped the scales in our favor. He was probably a better player than me, but while I concentrated on the game, he continued talking all the while. It didn't bother Paul or me, but it rattled Carol, and we took the first two sets easily.

Toward the end of the first game in the third set, I was tiring; I thought I was in good shape from running, but tennis required different muscles. I also found that my running shoes slowed me down because I couldn't pivot easily. I made a lunge for a ball, managed to get my racquet on it, then turned quickly. My body turned faster than my foot, and I fell down and twisted my ankle.

170

My scraped knee hurt more than my ankle at first, but mostly I just felt like a clumsy oaf. I started to get up, but Paul yelled for me to stay where I was. He knelt in front of me and gently felt my ankle for broken bones. Carol and Quentin came over to see if I was all right. Quentin started instructing Paul on what he should look for.

Paul helped me up. "There's nothing broken, but I think you should go into the clubhouse and soak it in some ice to get the swelling down. If you want, though, I can take you to get it X-rayed."

It wasn't the first time I had ever twisted an ankle, but it was the first time anyone had ever made such a fuss about it. I didn't know whether I liked it or not. But I'd had enough tennis, so Carol and I took off for the clubhouse and left the guys to battle it out on the court.

We sat and talked while I soaked my ankle, and then we changed into our bathing suits. The ice had numbed the ankle so that I felt very little pain walking out to the pool area. While we swam it didn't bother me at all.

I'm not great at tennis, but I'm a terrific swimmer, and the others had to finally drag me out of the pool. We hadn't eaten since breakfast and were all starved. Carol and I told the men we'd meet them in the dining room.

While we waited for the men Carol asked me whether I was spending the evening with Paul.

"Not that I know of. It was only going to be a game of tennis."

"Would you like to go somewhere your last night here?"

"No, I'm exhausted. I'd just like to spend a quiet evening at home." Also, my ankle was beginning to throb.

When Paul and Quentin joined us, the waiter brought over menus. They served only seafood or steak, and since we had eaten in a seafood restaurant the night before, everyone but Paul ordered steak. Carol and I ordered ours rare; Quentin ordered his well-done and lectured us on the dangers of eating undercooked meat. I found myself wondering if Carol could stand being lectured for the rest of her life.

The dinner was delicious. The steak was thick and charcoal broiled and was served with new potatoes and fresh asparagus. Paul had ordered lobster, which also looked delicious, so he shared some of it with me. Afterward we had coffee, and a waiter wheeled a pastry cart over to our table. Pastries were my downfall; one of the reasons I ran every day was so that I could indulge myself in sweets. I don't know the name for what I had, but I'll never forget how terrific it tasted.

We were relaxing over a second cup of coffee when Paul said to Carol, "Aren't those your parents over there?"

Carol turned and looked. "Yes. They must have been playing golf."

"Wonderful. I get to meet the whole family," crowed Quentin.

Carol gave him a wary look. "I really don't think it's necessary for you to meet everyone this trip."

Quentin looked like a little boy who had dropped his ice-cream cone. "But I *want* to meet them, Carol."

Carol lifted an eyebrow in my direction and sighed. "Will you excuse us for a minute?"

The check arrived while they were gone, and I watched Paul sign for it.

He saw me staring at his signature. "What is it?"

"Your handwriting seems so familiar."

"That's what you said when I wrote you the prescription. I forgot to ask. Have you been able to sleep any better?"

"Yes—thanks to you. I hate the idea of taking sleeping pills, but it sure is nice to get a full night's sleep."

"How's your ankle? Bothering you any?"

I had never been out with a doctor before, and I appreciated his concern. "It's hurting some, but I'll take a couple of asperins when I get home."

"Let me take a look at it."

I pushed my chair back from the table and crossed my sore ankle over my other leg for him to get a look. He touched it gently, and I winced.

"It's still swollen. I think you have a slight sprain. It's not serious, but sprains can be painful. Anyway, stay off it as much as possible during the next couple of days."

I was about to tell him I was flying to California the next day when Carol came back to the table alone. I looked over to where Quentin was sitting with her parents and saw that they were laughing at something he was saying. Carol sat down. "Listen, the folks want us to stop by their place for a couple of hours."

I grinned at her. "I take it they approve."

She rolled her eyes up to the ceiling. "He's got Dad convinced he's an authority on golf, and I think Mother is already planning the wedding. In her circles I'm considered a spinster. Anyway, they can drive us home later."

"I'll take Kathryn home in a few minutes," said Paul. "She needs to stay off that ankle tonight."

"Do you mind being alone with Rick, Katie?"

"Don't be silly, Carol. I'll be fine."

I walked to the Allison's table with her and Paul, and I said hello to them. They invited us over, too, but I said

I was tired, and Paul said he'd already made plans with some friends for later.

I was limping as we went out to the parking lot, and Paul put his arm around my waist and helped take some of the weight off my ankle.

"I think we should stop by my office on the way home, Kathryn. It really should be bandaged. It will feel a lot better if I do it for you." He opened the car door and helped me inside.

"I'd appreciate that, Paul, if you have the time."

"No problem," he assured me.

His medical suite was in a modern complex right outside of town. He took me into his office, and I sat behind his desk in a large leather chair while he went to get the bandages.

He had one of those desk calendars where you write in things to remember, and I was looking at it, not thinking of anything in particular, when I remembered where I had seen his writing before. It was his writing in the ledger book.

Without thinking, I pulled the calendar closer to get a better look. Yes, I was sure of it. It was the same handwriting.

I looked up and saw Paul staring down at me. Suddenly he didn't look pleasantly boyish anymore, and I began to feel afraid. I knew something of what I was thinking had shown in my face, because his eyes narrowed and a hard, cruel look came into them.

"So you finally remembered?" His voice was deadly calm.

"Remembered what?" I managed to say, hoping to bluff my way past his suspicions.

But he paid no attention to my innocent act. "When you

said the writing on my prescription looked familiar, I wondered. Then at dinner when I saw you staring at my signature . . ."

Katie, you idiot, I told myself, don't just sit there with your mouth hanging open. Use your wits. Play dumb. Convince him you know nothing. Because if you don't— but my mind didn't want to take it any further than that.

I laughed a bit shakily. "You're right, Paul. I was trying to figure out why your handwriting seemed so familiar. And then, here in the office, it came to me. It looks just like my father's. Only it has been so long since I have seen his writing. He died many years ago." It sounded completely fabricated, even to me, and I could tell I had not convinced him. "My ankle's really hurting now. Are you going to bandage it? Just an ace bandage would do—I've used them before, and they're terrific." Now I was blabbering like an idiot.

"Where's the book, Kathryn?"

"What book? What are you talking about?" I tried to stall for time, wondering how much to tell him. If I told him the police had it, he might kill me on the spot—he looked angry enough. I'd tell him I had it—that I'd have to take him to where I had hid it.

He put his hands on my injured ankle and twisted it. The pain was excruciating, and I screamed. I had always thought I was a brave person, but no more. If he twisted my ankle again, I'd tell him anything he wanted to know. I bit down on my lower lip and tried not to cry.

"Where is it?" His hands were still on my ankle, ready to twist it again.

"I hid it," I sobbed.

He released my ankle and sat down on the corner of his desk. He was still wearing his tennis clothes: white shorts and a light-blue knit shirt. His blond hair was tousled, and the hair on his arms and legs was bleached white by the sun. His skin was tanned and healthy looking. I noticed all that. He looked nice, not like a killer. But his eyes, his cool blue eyes, looked very dangerous.

"Where did you hide it, Kathryn?"

God help me, I had to make that part convincing. I knew my life depended on it. I looked him in the eyes. "On the beach. I put it in one of those plastic trash bags and buried it at the bottom of the steps." I let out a couple of sobs. "You see—I thought it was a list of men Susan had had affairs with and then blackmailed. I wanted to protect her reputation. It wasn't until I saw your calendar that I realized . . ."

He looked as though he believed me. I think the detail about the trash bag lent it some authenticity, made it convincing.

"Where exactly did you bury it?"

"Right at the bottom of the steps. Not very deeply—I just dug out a hole with my hands. What is that book, anyway?"

He gave me a thoughtful look. "Something your sister stole from me."

I didn't ask him anything else. I was afraid of learning more, afraid he'd decide I knew too much to live.

He stood up. "Come into the examining room. I'll fix up your ankle."

I followed him docilely, afraid not to do exactly as he said. I climbed up on the table and lay down, the pain in my ankle severe.

He was opening the drawers of a cabinet. I watched him, and when he turned around, I saw he held a hypodermic needle in his hand instead of a bandage.

176

I panicked and started to get off the table, but he was too quick and strong for me. In a matter of seconds he had pinned my body down and injected the needle in my arm.

"Don't move," he warned me. "If I inject too much, it will kill you."

Tears were streaming down my face. "It will probably kill me anyway."

"No, only make you numb. You'll be able to understand me, and talk in a fashion, but you won't be able to fight me. And, if you'll notice, you probably don't feel pain in your ankle anymore."

It was true. I no longer felt any pain in my ankle. I didn't even feel my ankle. Or my leg. Or any other part of my body. I tried to move my hand, but nothing happened. I could still think, but my body felt like it had been injected with a giant dose of Novocain.

"What did you . . . give me?" I could still talk, although it came out slower and a little slurred.

He was washing the hypodermic and putting it away. "It's called Pavulon, if that means anything to you."

It didn't, but I wanted to keep talking. I was afraid that if I didn't my mind would succumb to the drug the way my body had. And maybe if that happened, I would die. Then I realized I was just fooling myself. Of course he would kill me. How could he leave me alive to tell of his twisting my ankle, and injecting me with a drug. And I realized, too, that he must have killed my sister.

That meant Rick was innocent. And if Rick was innocent, there was no reason why we—Oh, God, I didn't want to die. I wanted to live—to be able to love Rick.

"You're going to kill me, aren't you?"

He laughed. "So you finally figured that out, did you?"

"You won't get away with it. Everyone knows I'm with you."

He came over and stood by the table, calmly drying his hands with a towel. "On the contrary, everything worked out perfectly for me. Carol and Quentin will say I drove you home. Rick is there all alone. Everyone, including you, thought Rick murdered your sister. Carol even asked if you'd be all right alone with him tonight. So when your body is found in the same spot where they found Susan, whom do you think they will suspect? No, my dear, everything points to my good friend Rick."

He was right. Everything did point to Rick. Even if Tony finally got Paul for the drug business, that wouldn't necessarily connect him to the murders. With a shock I realized I'd used murder in the plural. In my mind I already had myself dead. No, I refused to give up that easily. At least I could try to delay him, ask him some questions. He was probably eager for someone to know how clever he had been. If I could gain enough time, perhaps Carol and Quentin would get home earlier. I just couldn't give up hope and go to my death without a struggle. Perhaps I could no longer put up a physical fight, but my mind was still functioning.

"Was it you who searched my room?"

"Yes. And I did everything else, including fixing your brakes. I wanted you to leave, go home, quit meddling! If it hadn't been for you, Susan's death would have been accepted as a suicide."

"I have a reservation for tomorrow."

"You were finally leaving? Giving up?"

"Yes. I was convinced Rick had done it, but there was no evidence."

178

"So, if we hadn't played tennis today . . . oh, well, you can't win them all."

He dismissed my life with such ease. "If I promise not to tell anyone what you've done, couldn't—"

"It's too late for that, Kathryn."

I was sorry I had even asked. I would not beg him for my life. If I had to die, I wanted to go with some dignity.

"Why did you kill Susan?"

He let out a harsh laugh. "That bitch? She deserved to die. We had a business thing going together, and everything was running smoothly. Then your sweet sister stole my ledger book and threatened to expose me if I didn't pay her ten thousand dollars. Cauley is my home, Kathryn. I have a good medical practice here. I couldn't let her destroy that. And she wouldn't have stopped with ten thousand. It would have been ten thousand more, then fifteen thousand. It would have gone on forever."

"No, I don't think so," I said.

"What do *you* know about it?"

"She was planning to run away with Mike Campbell— to Italy. I think she just wanted the ten thousand for the trip."

He was silent for a minute. "Perhaps. But your sister loved money much more than she was capable of loving a man. No, I think she would have wanted more."

I was running out of questions and tried to think of something else to ask him.

"The wig—where did you get the blond wig?"

He gave me a measured look. "Time's up, Kathryn. It's dark enough now to leave."

I had thought I was so clever in delaying him, while all the time he had been waiting for it to get dark.

He looked carefully around the room, then picked up

179

my limp body and carried me out to the car. He laid me down on the backseat while tears of frustration ran unheeded down my face. It was terrifying being so completely helpless. I felt as if my head had been severed from my body. And even that was getting fuzzy. I felt it would be so easy just to close my eyes and allow my head to join my body in the numbness.

He drove fast, and it wasn't very long before he stopped the car and got out. He pulled me roughly from the backseat and slung me over his shoulder like a sack.

"Where are we?" I thought we'd be at Rick's house, but nothing looked familiar.

"On the edge of the Fowler property. They have an easier path down to the beach."

My last hope had been that Rick might look out the window and see Paul carrying me across the yard. I should have known Paul would be smarter than that.

Even after all the tennis and the swimming, he seemed to carry me downhill with no effort. The moon was out, and he could see his way clearly on the beach. It wasn't long before we reached the bottom of the steps.

He dumped my body unceremoniously on the sand and got down on his knees to dig for the book. It was about then that I realized I wasn't completely helpless. I could scream, but not on the beach against the sound of the waves. He intended to throw me from the spot where Susan had gone over. I would wait until we were almost there, and then I'd scream. I was sure one scream would be all the opportunity I'd have.

I heard him swear under his breath. "There's no book here. Where the hell is it?"

"I gave it to Tony Greco." It no longer mattered if he knew the truth.

180

There was a long silence. I couldn't see his face from where he dropped me, but I finally heard him sigh.

"No matter. There's nothing to connect me with the book. Or the book to my business. Your sister was my only link to those names. If Greco knew anything, he'd have picked me up by now. Rick's still the murder suspect."

He picked me up again. "I'm glad now that you're going to die. I was sorry to have to kill you before, but now that I find you lied to me . . . tried to trick me . . ."

I attempted to make my mind a blank as he carried me up the steps. I would not say a word to him—not one more word. I would make my one scream, but I had no hope of that saving me; I only hoped someone might hear it and Paul would be caught.

When at last he stopped, I knew we were at the point where he had killed Susan. I opened my mouth to scream, heard a familiar voice say, "Hold it right there, Sanders," and then Paul dropped me, and that's the last I remembered.

Chapter Sixteen

When I regained consciousness, I was in a hospital, and Tony Greco and a doctor were standing by my bed.

The doctor was holding my wrist, taking my pulse.

Tony was watching me. "Do you know who I am, Katie?"

I tried to speak but nothing came out. I nodded my head yes, then winced at the pain.

"You have five minutes," the doctor told Tony before leaving the room.

Tony sat down on the edge of the bed and took my hand. "You're going to be okay, Katie. There won't be any aftereffects from the drug. It's already worn off, but when Sanders dropped you, you fell down those stone steps. Now don't get scared, you're going to be all right, but you won't be your usual pretty self for a while. You had a concussion, two of your ribs were broken, and your ankle is sprained. I understand from Carol that the sprain might have happened prior to your fall, though. You also have numerous cuts and bruises, and one of your eyes is black. So, if you think you can live with all that—"

When he saw my smile, a look of relief came over his face.

"Oh, yes, I can live with that." My vocal chords felt

rusty, but I had managed to talk. "I didn't think I was going to live at all. What about Paul? Did he give up without a struggle?"

Tony seemed to be watching me carefully. "He's dead, Katie. When he dropped you, he tripped and went over the side. A freak accident—went right over the guardrail. Broke his neck."

I thought how ironic it was that he died from the same injury as my sister. Poetic justice, really.

He leaned over and kissed me on the nose. "My five minutes are up, but I'll be back to tell you all the details."

As soon as he left I began to wonder where Rick was. He hadn't killed my sister. He hadn't done any of the things I had suspected him of doing, and there was no reason now for us not to be together. I couldn't wait to see him, to tell him how I felt. Perhaps the hospital had rules about visitors and he hadn't been allowed in.

Tony stopped by later in the day. By then I had seen myself in a mirror a nurse had held up for me, and I realized what an act of bravery it had been for him to kiss me. My nose was about the only place on me that wasn't bruised. But they would all heal—the bruises and the ribs and the ankle. I was alive, and I'd never take that fact for granted again.

Tony told me how he had recognized the writing on the prescription as soon as he had picked it up. The man he had sent to fill the prescription had taken it to the lab, where it had been identified as having been written by the same person who wrote in the ledger book.

"But I wouldn't have had enough evidence to take to court, Katie, without the information Johnny Fowler gave me. It seems that Shel knew someone who had actually dealt directly with Sanders. We got to the guy, and he said he'd testify if we granted him immunity. Of course, that's academic now."

After talking to Johnny Fowler, Tony had spent a long time questioning Rick. He told me that what had finally made him suspect Rick was when I told him Rick was the only one who knew I was driving to Boston. I had forgotten that I had mentioned it when Paul was there. He said they went over every incident that had occurred, and Paul was always on the scene. And Rick, hearing his old friend was selling drugs, no longer felt any loyalty toward him.

"I got upset, Katie, when he said you were out with Paul, but Rick was certain that you were perfectly safe with Quentin and Carol along. Later, though, Carol called Rick from the Allison's home, and when Rick found out you were alone with Paul, and that you should have been home long before, he called me immediately. We had a call out to every squad car to watch for Paul's car. We had his home staked out and also Rick's. Finally a car spotted him heading for Rick's, and we all converged at that point. But, of course, we know now he parked near the Fowler's and took you down that way."

I smiled at him. "But you got there in time. The most beautiful sound I've ever heard was your voice saying, 'Hold it right there, Sanders.' "

He looked pleased. "That got to you, huh?"

"My hero!" I told him, and I swear the man blushed.

I remained in the hospital for five days. Carol came to visit me and talked at length about that nightmarish Saturday night: "When I called and told Rick that Quentin and I were visiting the folks, he was frantic. 'Why did you leave her alone with Paul?' he shouted at me, but I didn't know what he was so upset about. I never even considered Paul as the murderer, did you?"

"Not until it was too late," I admitted ruefully.

She looked saddened. "It's still hard to believe. He was always like one of the family. The drugs—well, I can understand greed, I guess. But to involve his best friend's wife and then kill her. All for money." She shook her head in resignation.

"Were you there when—"

"When he tried to kill you? No, we arrived when the medics were carrying you up the steps on a stretcher, Tony by your side. He had tears in his eyes, Katie. But I guess we all did."

I tried to visualize Tony with tears in his eyes, but the image wouldn't materialize. I wanted to ask her about Rick. Did he have tears in his eyes, too? But I couldn't. Some stubborn pride prevented me from asking.

"And, oh, Katie, you should have seen Quentin. He was shouting orders to the police and the ambulance attendants and just generally directing traffic. Tony just watched him for a while, then allowed him to continue."

I chuckled at her description. "Are you going to marry him, Carol?"

"I don't seem to have any choice in the matter. Everyone, including Quentin, just assumes I will."

"His, uh, verbosity won't bother you?"

"Of course it will. But I figure if we have several children, he'll space it out between us, and then it won't be so bad. Tell me, Katie, do you feel more at peace about your sister's death now?"

"Yes, I think so. Suicide—well, that would have been unthinkable. And if she had caused such hatred in her marriage that her husband killed her, I would have found that difficult to understand. But she was taking risks getting involved with dealing drugs. And she *was* blackmailing Paul. So, in a sense, she took her chances and lost. Nonetheless, it seems such a waste."

She left before I had summoned up the courage to ask her about Rick. I couldn't understand why he didn't come to see me. I was sure he had felt the same way I had that night on the beach. But maybe I had built things up all out of proportion in my mind, just as I had after meeting him for the first time in California. He probably had no intentions of getting involved again so soon. I tried not to think of him but found that impossible.

Mrs. Gurney came to visit and talked about Sara. "The little one misses you. She thought at first you had gone back to California without saying good-bye to her, but we explained you were sick and in the hospital. I told her I was coming to see you today, and she wanted to come along, but the hospital doesn't allow children to visit."

"The way I look, I'd probably scare her anyway."

"You wouldn't scare anyone, miss. Everybody's crazy about you. Why, Mr. Allison and Sara talk about you all the time."

I wanted to ask her what Rick said about me. If he talked about me all the time, why didn't he come to see me? But I kept silent.

Mike Campbell came to visit me. His big, booming presence brightened up the room. He wanted to know everything that had happened, and I answered all his questions.

"You look like hell, Katie, but you've sure got guts. How about running away with me to Rome?"

"If I said yes, you'd probably have a heart attack."

"Try me."

186

I shook my head and smiled.

"You think I'm kidding, but I'm not. I'd like to get to know you better—you're my kind of woman."

"I'm really not like my sister."

"The expression 'my kind of woman' in my case covers a lot of categories," he said, then had to leave.

The next day a package was delivered to me at the hospital. When I opened it, it contained a miniature in marble of the unicorn in his studio. But still Rick didn't come, and I had no word from him.

The Allisons came to visit and talked about Carol and Quentin.

"He's just right for Carol," said Mr. Allison. "Did you know he was a champion golfer?"

"I'll be happy to see Carol settled down at last," Mrs. Allison added, beaming with happiness. They didn't mention Rick at all, nor did I.

Quentin came to visit and talked, and talked. And then said a few more things. Looking past his shoulder, I saw that a group of nurses had gathered outside my door and were listening to him with rapt faces. But with all his talking, he never mentioned Rick to me. Not once.

The night before I was due to be released, Tony came by again. He pulled a chair up close to my bed and sat looking down at me, a serious expression on his face.

"Why so glum?" I teased him. "I'm sure you've become the local hero."

"I hear you're flying back to California tomorrow."

I nodded. Rick had not come to see me once, not even called. I didn't want to be an embarrassment to him by being at his house any longer, since he obviously had no desire to see me, so I had made a reservation home.

Tony avoided my eyes. "Would you reconsider, Katie?

Would you stay here and marry me? I love you, you know."

"Oh, Tony," I said, reaching out my arms to him. As I put them around his neck I saw someone move out of the doorway. Whoever it was probably thought he was interrupting a romantic scene. "You don't love me, Tony. People always feel like that when they save someone's life."

He gave me a crooked grin. "In other words, you're trying to let me down gently."

I sighed. "Yeah, I guess so. I like you. I'm sure you know that. But—"

"But no fireworks go off when you're with me."

"Something like that."

We said our good-byes, and I was sorry that I couldn't return his feelings. At least he loved me. Being in love with someone who didn't care wasn't doing much for my ego.

The rest of the evening passed slowly. I kept thinking, against all hope, that maybe Rick would still show up. But he still hadn't when the night nurse came to give me a sleeping pill and turn out the lights.

Chapter Seventeen

Carol picked me up the next morning to drive me home to pack before taking me to the airport. My ankle felt all right, and my ribs only hurt when I laughed. Nevertheless, the hospital insisted on my traveling out to the parking lot in a wheelchair.

"You've become notorious, Katie," Carol said to me as we drove off.

"Notorious?"

"Truly. The local papers had the story, naturally, but then the wire services picked it up. 'Sister of well-known writer's wife,' etc., etc. You know how it goes—anything for a little sensationalism."

I thought of my friends back home reading about me. They had never thought I was the type to have any sort of adventures, and I would have been the first to agree with them. "My students are going to think I'm quite the heroine," I joked, and we both laughed.

"What happened with you and Rick, Katie? He sure looked glum when he got home last night, and I was afraid to ask."

"Nothing's happened with us—he never came to see me in the hospital."

"Well, he kept asking everyone if you had asked about

him, but you hadn't. I thought he went by to see you last night."

"No, the only one who came by last night was Tony."

"Ummm. He's a sweetheart, isn't he?"

"Tony?"

"Yes."

"Yes, he is." I was sorry I wouldn't be seeing Tony again, or Carol, or the others. Maybe getting away from Massachusetts, from the house, would cheer me up. Maybe back in California I'd be able, at last, to forget Rick.

Mrs. Gurney and Sara were at the door to greet me when we arrived. I wanted to pick up Sara and give her a hug but was afraid of damaging my mending ribs, so Mrs. Gurney picked her up so that I could give the child a kiss without bending over.

"Do you need any help packing?" Carol asked me, but I said no. I was near tears at the thought of my departure and wanted a little time to myself.

I slowly eased myself up the stairway, then went down the hall to my room. There wasn't much to pack, and I had decided not to take any of Susan's belongings back with me. The fewer reminders the better, I thought.

I heard a knock and turned around. Rick was standing outside the room, looking very tired and drawn.

"I wanted to say good-bye. I hadn't thought you'd be leaving so soon, but Carol told me yesterday that you had made reservations."

"Yes. I thought it was time I went home." In my mind I was praying that he'd ask me to stay, while at the same time accepting the fact that he wasn't going to or he would have done so sooner.

"But you'll be back, of course."

"I'd like to keep in touch with Sara. But that probably won't be for some time."

He looked surprised. "Oh, is Tony going out to California?"

Now it was my turn to look surprised. "Not that I know of. Why?"

"Aren't you two getting married?"

I must have looked as perplexed as I felt. "Me and Tony?"

"Yes."

"Where did you get that idea?"

"I went by the hospital to see you last night, and—"

I remembered the man in the doorway whom I had briefly glimpsed as I had held out my arms to Tony. "And you heard him propose?"

He nodded.

"Well, if you hadn't rushed off, you would have heard my refusal."

"Tony's a good man." Rick came into the room and watched as I packed my few remaining things.

"Yes, he is," I agreed. "But I don't love him." The fact that he had come to see me, although belatedly, I thought, was giving me hope.

"Well, you know what they say about eavesdroppers," he said with a shaky laugh before lapsing into silence.

I realized then I would have to take the initiative with him. "I'm glad you came, anyway, even if I didn't get to see you."

He smiled, and it traveled from his lips up to his eyes, warming his whole face. "I didn't know if you wanted to see me."

How could I tell him that I had thought of little else during my stay in the hospital; that he had been on my mind from the time I was awakened in the morning until I fell asleep at night. "I wanted to see you, Rick."

He came over to me and took my face very gently in his hands. "I love you, Kathryn; with all my heart, I love you."

Tears of happiness streamed down my face. "Oh, Rick, I love you, too. I always have."

"Kathryn, will you tell me something?"

"Anything!"

"Why didn't you know instinctively that I wasn't a murderer?"

I raised an eyebrow. "Why didn't you know instinctively that my sister wasn't me?"

"Touché! Tell me, Kathryn, are we going to let our rotten instincts affect our chance of happiness together?"

"Oh, I hope not, Rick." I put my arms around his neck, careful not to strain my ribs.

"Then you'll marry me?"

"When?"

He laughed. "You're supposed to say yes, not when."

"Yes."

"As for when, we'll have to see. I should observe a proper period of mourning. Not that my family and friends wouldn't understand, but we don't want to give the scandalmongers any more ammunition."

"I've signed a teaching contract for next year, anyway."

"What a lot of nonsense—as though I could wait an entire year!"

Before I could get any words in about the legality of contracts, he had effectively silenced me by closing his mouth over mine. Just before I closed my eyes and gave myself over to his kiss, I caught a glimpse of three beaming faces in the doorway before they disappeared down the hall.